The **THREADS** Which Bind us

Casey Halston

The Threads which Bind us
Casey Halston
© 2022 Oxford eBooks Ltd.
Published under the sci-fi-cafe.com imprint.
www.oxford-ebooks.com

ISBN 978-1-910779-98-9 (Paperback)

sci-fi-cafe.com

PROLOGUE

HIM

BEFORE HER VOICE called, there was nothing, not even a dream-state. Drifting without motion, though space without dimension, I had come from another place long forgotten.

But I was drawn back into existence because I needed to be in the world again, and I was needed.

Then her eyes, lit up only by the moonlight streaming through her open window. Flickering open for a moment to sweep over me, then closing again with sleep.

Now I was here, but all I was, was now, a razor-thin part of all that I had been, like a soap bubble in time.

CHAPTER 1

ANNA

THE FIRST TIME he visited me, I hadn't got out of bed in two days.

It was 10 o'clock on a Tuesday when I woke, which meant I had missed my 9am Poetry Class. I was sure it wouldn't come as a surprise to my tutor or any of my classmates, since I was an irregular attendee at university anyway.

Autumn was coming to an end, and it had been one that seemed to shake the leaves from every tree, rendering them barren and empty, ready for winter. My room looked like it had been recently devastated by a natural disaster – a tornado, or some sort of landslide that had caused my books to scatter across the floor. I didn't bother checking my phone as I sat up, knowing that it was most likely dead – I'd forgotten to charge it again. I toyed with the idea of climbing out of bed and getting in the shower, but even the thought of it seemed to drain me. I pushed my dark fringe out of my eyes and cringed when I realised how dry it felt against my fingers.

"Ugh, fine." I muttered to no-one in particular, rolling out of bed ungracefully and stumbling in the direction of the bathroom.

I brushed my teeth, inspecting myself in the mirror as I did so. The last month had taken its toll on me and my skin looked slightly paler than it normally was, making the green of my eyes seem darker than usual. I was pleased to see there were no bags under my eyes, despite the fact that my sleep had lately been light and often interrupted. The bathroom tiles were cold on my feet and when I had finished brushing my teeth, I went to turn back to my room to put the radiator on.

I saw the colour of him first. That pale sort of sheen, more silver than it was grey. When my eyes passed over it, I almost mistook it for a cloud of wispy smoke, settling unnaturally over my desk chair. But when I focused properly, I saw that it wasn't that at all. It was a person.

My breath caught in my throat and I couldn't close my mouth. I stared and they – no, *he* – stared back. The light from my window was shining *through* him. God, how could it be shining through him? I thought I must be hallucinating, so I blinked hard, but when I opened my eyes again, he was still there. Sitting on my desk chair, looking at me. Looking at me with eyes that weren't even there. I drew a deep breath in and went to–

"Please don't scream," he said. He *spoke*. I stumbled back against the sink, breathing shallow breaths now, still completely unable to form a sentence, or even a sound. The form raised its hands. "Honestly, I'm just as confused as you are. Please," His voice softened, imploring me, "just don't scream."

And then he was quiet again. A translucent man sat on my desk chair, *looking* at me, *talking* to me. I shook my head and tried to rationalise the whole thing.

"I'm… dreaming." I stuttered, more to myself than

to the illusory figure. I looked down at my hands in front of me, trying to decide whether they looked real or not.

"Maybe," he replied, nodding his silver head in a seemingly sincere motion, "you could try pinching yourself?"

"Yes! Yeah…" I said and squeezed the skin on my forearm hard between my thumb and finger. The skin went white, then red when the blood flowed back. I looked back up towards the desk chair, willing the figure to be gone, for this to all have been some sleep-induced error.

But he was still there, quiet and still, and see-through. He cocked his head.

"Are you waking up?" he asked quietly.

I screwed my eyes shut tightly, shaking my head and folding myself down until I was sat on the floor of my bathroom, the cold tiles uncomfortable on my thighs.

"I've gone mental, I've actually gone mental. I *must* be going mad… I can't… What else…" I eventually trailed off and opened my eyes again.

He hadn't moved from the chair. I took a deep breath to try and steady the jitters that I could feel coming on. I could see the books on my shelf behind him, *through him*. At first I had thought that he had no colour to him at all, only the strange paleness, but now I saw that this wasn't completely true. There was a tiny amount of human colour to him, enough to distinguish the pale of his skin with the darkness of his hair, but his eyes were completely grey. The way that the light shone through him seemed to suggest that his body was moving even when it wasn't, and as he sat completely still, watching me watching him, it almost looked as though the skin – *skin?* – on his arms was drifting a little. He was wearing some sort of clothing, but it was hard to make out exactly what it was against the harsh natural light of the window. We stared at each other, it seemed for minutes.

"I–" he started, but I interrupted before he could finish.

"*No.*" I managed, trying my hardest to keep my voice firm and steady, even though I felt like the entire room was about to start spinning. "Don't talk. I talk. I ask questions. Okay?"

He nodded and I stood up, still leaning up against the sink, unwilling to take even a single step towards him.

"How did you get here?" I began, unable yet to ask the question that I really wanted to. He seemed to take a deep breath and shift a little in the chair.

"I don't…" he trailed off for a moment, then started again, shaking his head as he spoke, "I'm sorry, I don't really know. I can't remember, I just… This is where I am, I don't know how."

I laughed humourlessly; it came out as more of a bark. "Well, did you walk through the front door and come into my room?"

I think he might have frowned for a moment, though it was hard to tell, but then he started shaking his head. "No. No I definitely didn't come through the house. I don't even know what it looks like. Or *where* we are. I'm just… here." He sighed, then put his head down, not looking at me. "I'm sorry, I know this is–"

"*No.*" I put my hands up in protest, stopping him.

"No. Okay. Fine. You don't know. Next question. Um."
I rested my head in my palms and closed my eyes for
a moment. "Oh God, okay. Who… are you?" I tried
uncertainly, opening one eye to squint at the figure of
him across the room.

"I'm sorry. I don't know that either–" he started, but
again I stopped him.

"*What do you mean, you don't know?*" I growled,
through gritted teeth. "How can you *not know* who
you are?" I glared at him now.

He shifted around again uncomfortably, not meeting
my eyes. "I know this must be scary for you–"

"*Scary* for me?!" I snapped. "You mean, to have
someone – some*thing* just show up in my room–"

"Okay," he said, his voice louder and harsher than it
had been before, "I *know*, but it's strange for me too,
okay? I don't know either, I don't know why – or, *who*
– sorry, I'm–"

"What are you?!" I finally managed to blurt out,
stopping him in his spiral of confusion.

The skies had clouded behind him, taking the light
out of the room and out of him. The grey in his eyes
seemed to darken and he cleared his throat a little, but
he didn't answer. Maybe he couldn't.

I don't know why, but I took a small step towards
him.

HIM

She took a step towards me. Granted, it was a small
step. But still, a good sign.

I tried to answer her questions, but I couldn't. The
truth is, I was just as clueless about what was going on

as she was. I couldn't remember *anything* before last night and I certainly couldn't remember walking into this poor girl's house. I didn't know where I was, who she was... even who *I* was. And at that moment, I was honestly barely keeping it together.

I looked down again at my hands, like I had done maybe a dozen times since the beginning of this strange experience. They were translucent – not entirely, of course, but enough to see the girl's wooden floorboards through them. Enough to be abnormal. From her reaction, it seemed that my whole body must look the same way, though I hadn't been able to muster the willpower to look in the mirror yet. God, the way she was looking at me. Eyes wide, skin drained of any colour, still holding back the urge to shake, even now. Like she'd seen...

A ghost? Like she'd seen a ghost. Of course, this was the most logical option (if logical can even be used in this scenario). But I knew that neither of us could bring ourselves to say it. To say it aloud, to actually admit it was to open a door that neither of us could walk back through, me especially.

Ghost? To... be dead? Caught in some in-between? To have once been alive... but have absolutely no memory of it? God, *why* can't I remember? Thinking back felt like walking blindly down a dark corridor, with absolutely nothing to guide me. No light, no reference points. Just nothing.

And the *feeling* of it, here, being in this room. Just, being. It felt strange, like I was half in the room and half somewhere else completely. Somewhere unknown. I could feel the sensation of the chair underneath me as

I sat on it, could feel the wood touching my legs, but the pressure was soft, like at any minute I might fall through it entirely.

Earlier that morning, when the girl had been asleep and I'd found myself in her room, I'd tried to pick up a pen from the desk which I was sat at now. The pen had laid on my flat, open palm for only half a minute, before it breached the surface of me and tumbled through my hand, clattering to the floor, making the girl stir a little in her slumber. And there were no feelings *inside* of me, it was like everything inside of me was completely hollow. I felt no need to breathe in or out, but had kept doing so purely by instinct. I could not feel my lungs filling up and then emptying again. I could not feel my heartbeat.

I couldn't think about it too deeply. Each time I let myself, I felt like the walls were going to start closing in on me. Like I was going to start hyperventilating, with lungs I potentially didn't even have. I had to focus on the situation at hand and what I *did* know.

I was there. In a room. With a girl, who I didn't know. Who was looking at me like I was, potentially, a monster.

"I'm not here to hurt you, or pry..." I started, not really knowing where I was even going with it.

I really *didn't* want to hurt her, I just wanted the same thing she did – to figure out what was going on and how exactly it had come to be. But she was looking at me like she needed answers and though I couldn't blame her for that, I was wracked with guilt, because I couldn't give them to her.

"Why *are* you here?" she replied after a while, in

a small voice. I heaved a deep breath, that I didn't actually need. I didn't know what to say, and even when a fractured thought entered my head, I knew it was nothing that she would want to hear.

"I don't know." I said, my tone apologetic.

She frowned, which in some ways was much better than the expressions she'd had up until now – fear, shock and possibly disgust. When she frowned her face softened a little and I could see some of the colour coming back to her skin. She had these deep green eyes, that seemed to get darker towards the centre. Like some sort of whirlpool. But there was no trust in those eyes that I could see, even though the fear seemed to be subsiding slightly.

"You don't believe me?" I said, attempting to read her mind through her expression.

"No, I..." She shook her head, squeezing her eyes shut under dark, thick eyelashes. "Ugh, I don't know, okay? I mean, why should I believe you? I don't know you. I don't even know..." She trailed off, bringing a shaky hand up to gesture at me. At my barely human body. "*What* you are... I don't..."

She threw her head back and let out a disgruntled shout. I resisted the urge to stand up from the chair and approach her, because as much as I wanted to be reassuring, I was almost certain that it would come across as creepy. She fixed me with a steady stare again. Despite everything, I couldn't help but feel like she was actually handling this quite well.

"Tell me what you *do* know. You must know something."

I sighed again. "I appeared here. I didn't come

through the house, I just materialised in the room," I said, gesturing over to the left side of the head of her bed, next to the bathroom door, "there. I don't know why–"

"When?" She interrupted me, making me lose my train of thought for a moment.

"What?" I asked. She was looking at me expectantly.

"When? When did you..." She raised her hands and made air-quotes, "'materialise'?"

I paused for a moment.

"I mean," she went on, "I'm assuming you've been here for a while, since before I woke up, but I didn't see you last night–"

She didn't remember seeing me last night.

"No," I interrupted her this time, "this morning. Maybe an hour before you woke up. It was still light outside." A lie. She frowned and I dreaded her pressing me further on it.

"So, you were just... here, while I was... sleeping?!" Her voice was rising and getting louder as she spoke and I could tell that she was getting angry, rightfully so.

"I know, I know. I'm sorry, but would you rather I'd woken you up?" I asked, trying not to sound too harsh.

She pondered this for a moment, then brought her hand to her face and rubbed her forehead like she was trying to relieve some pressure.

"God, no. Definitely not." she muttered, I think more to herself than to me. "Why didn't you just *leave*?" she asked, and I tried not to flinch at her words.

Of course, I had tried that this morning. When I saw

the clock stood on her mantelpiece beginning to get closer to 9 o'clock, a deep panic had started to set in. What was going to happen when she woke up? What the hell would she think, what would she say? What if she tried to attack me, or scream for help and her huge terrifying father had walked through the door with a gun, or a baseball bat? Although thinking about that now, neither of those things would likely have any impact on me, in the state I was currently in. Still, overcome with anxiety, I had tried to open the door to her bedroom, but each time I had put pressure on the door handle, it would pull down a fraction, but then my glassy hand would pass right through it, like the pen had passed through me earlier.

"I can't, um..." I brought my hands to my face, rubbing it and noting how gentle the sensation felt, "I can't actually open the, uh... Ugh, the door. I tried, but I couldn't..." I stood then, deciding it was probably best to do a small demonstration, rather than try to explain the obviously impossible.

I picked an earring from her desk behind me, a small dangly golden dream-catcher shape and held it in my open palm in front of me for her to see. She looked at the earring in my hand, then back to me, like I was a complete madman. Then, the earring fell to the floor, passing through my hand. Her jaw dropped open.

"What the–"

"I know." I said, shaking my head and bending to pick up the earring from the floor, then quickly placing it back on the desk before it could fall again. "When I touch things, they'll stay where I hold them for a little while, but if I put too much pressure on an object, it'll just..." I shrugged and laughed nervously.

"Pass *through you?*" She almost squealed, in complete disbelief of what she had just seen.

"Well," I cleared my throat, even though I didn't need to, "in theory, it makes sense–"

"*MAKES SENSE?*" she screeched, her face now flushed and her green eyes turning wild. "What do you *mean? Nothing* about this makes sense." She stormed past me, to her bedroom door, which I'd not too long ago failed to open and launched the door open so hard that it smacked the wall. Then she turned back to me.

"Please," she said, through gritted teeth, "I'm sorry, but please, just go. The back door will be open, it always is, you can leave through there."

She folded her arms across her chest and looked at me sternly. She looked tired, but not the kind of tired that a good night's sleep would be able to fix. She looked wild and angry and frightened, and tired.

Now that she was awake and speaking to me, looking at me. I was sure that she probably feared me, maybe even hated me, and that made me incredibly anxious, but... It was nothing compared to the anxiety that the thought of going out, into the world, brought on.

I didn't even know *where I was*. I didn't know where to go, and even if I did, I wouldn't know *how* to get there. And what the hell would happen once *others* saw me? I shuddered inwardly at the thought.

"But, I–" I started.

"Please." she pleaded, and something softer appeared in her eyes now. Not fear, or hate.

I realised then that she couldn't handle me being

there with her. So, it wasn't fair that I stay. I had to go.

I nodded and walked toward the open door. I quickly glanced in her direction as I passed her, but she was not looking at me anymore. Her steely gaze was directed the desk, where I'd stood before. When I reached the doorway, I took a deep breath and went to step through.

But I was met with resistance. More resistance than I could remember having felt before. I frowned and tried again, this time not just stepping, but *forcing* myself forward – pushing through the resistance with flat palms up against the open doorway. But something was *blocking* me. Something that I couldn't even *see*. It was as if I was pointlessly pushing, with all of my power, against a solid wall, even though there was no wall there to be seen. I shoved and shoved, but to no avail.

I could not walk through the door.

I turned back to the girl. She was stood still, arms hanging limply by her sides, green eyes wide with incredulity.

"I... I can't..." I stuttered.

Her voice came out barely above a whisper.

"You can't leave, can you?"

"My name is Anna," she explained, sat on top of her bedspread, legs crossed underneath her. "Anna Wilder."

Had she not been staring at me so intently, green eyes fixated on my face, making me feel extremely self-conscious, I think I might have smiled at her name. Wilder seemed extremely fitting, somehow.

I took a moment to observe her, *really* observe her, without feeling worried that my gaze might cause her discomfort, or fear.

Actually, she was quite something to look at. Incredibly dark, almost black, hair framed her face and fell past her shoulders, flicking outwards at the ends and completely covering her back. Her skin, in comparison, was very pale and was made to seem even more so by the smatterings of light brown freckles that fell across the bridge of her nose and her cheeks. Her eyes were huge almond shapes, making them almost impossible not to stare at. They were unlike any green I could recognise – so deep and dark in the middle that they nearly blended into the black of her pupils, but so light on the outer rims that they seemed almost olive coloured.

Sat closed-up like this, she seemed tiny. But I'd seen from the way she'd stood earlier that there was nothing meek or timid about her. She spoke with conviction, even now, when she was as unsure as she was.

"Thank you, for telling me." I said, trying to sound as gentle as I could. "And, um… Where are we? I mean, is this your family house, or…" I was still fighting the nagging fear that her dad might come in at any minute, swinging his fists. But she was shaking her head.

"Not family, no," she replied, "I live here with two other girls from university. One of them, Hannah, she's studying abroad for a term. Samantha might be here, but she stays with her boyfriend a lot, I don't really…" She took a sharp breath and rubbed her eyes with her fists for a moment. I didn't interrupt her. "I haven't really been great at staying in touch with them recently." she finished, her voice hard and firm.

I decided not to push it, since she seemed to have put up some sort of wall. In all honesty, I was just grateful that I wouldn't be having any frightening encounters with family members any time soon. There was so much else to get used to, before even considering all of that.

She was at university. Looking at her now, it made complete sense. She looked about student-age and it had seemed odd that she'd been completely free to sleep in until 10am with almost no disturbances and nobody coming to check on her. From a quick sweep of her room, I could deduce that she was most probably a literature student, as her floor was littered with what I recognised to be the classics.

"Literature?" I asked, gesturing at a particularly dog-eared copy of *To the Lighthouse* sat atop her desk. I was stood by the doorway, still unsure of where to place myself in her room.

She nodded. "With a minor in Philosophy." I stored this information away in my mind, keen to build up my memory, which for the moment remained painfully empty.

"And... where exactly are we?" I asked, "Uh, in the country, or, world? I guess, I mean..." I grimaced at the question. I was extremely wary of asking anything that might unsettle her, but I needed as much information as possible.

Her facial expression changed, but I couldn't read what it was yet. "Bridgwater... Um, England." she laughed, but there wasn't much humour in it.

"Oh, right." I said, because I didn't know what else to say. Truthfully, nothing that she said was ringing any bells in my head.

"You're English, too," she said abruptly, "I can tell. Your voice, I mean, your accent."

"Right, yeah of course." I said, shaking my head. God, she was *really* looking at me. I suppose I couldn't blame her.

"You really don't remember *anything?*" she whispered incredulously, tapping her fingers on her knee as she spoke. "And why can't you *leave?* I can't understand – I mean, can you–"

I screwed my eyes shut, taking shallower breaths now, trying my best to keep calm. "No, nothing." I replied. My voice had come out very quiet and hollow.

Something started ringing suddenly, snapping me out of my existentialism with a fright. Her phone, lit up beside her bed, was ringing incessantly. We stared at each other for a moment. Would she answer it? Would she tell whoever it was to come over, immediately? Would she cry down the phone, or whisper that someone was here to hurt her? She broke eye contact and leaned over to grab her phone. A sharp feeling of panic came over me and I opened my mouth to say something–

"It's my dad." she said almost blankly, staring at her phone with no expression. Then, she pressed a button to turn it off, or silence it somehow. I let out a sigh of relief, then grimaced when she snapped her head up to look at me.

"What?" she retorted harshly.

"I just, I thought that you might–"

"What," she laughed with no humour again, "I might tell my dad that I'm... what, exactly? Sat opposite a – with you, here? And have him call me insane? Or call a *doctor* for me?"

I frowned at her. It seemed like an overly-harsh reaction to the situation, to me. I was sure that if she had sounded sincere, any concerned parent would have at least checked up on her, or taken her seriously, at least to some degree? I couldn't see how any parent wouldn't want to make sure she was safe, regardless of how ridiculous the circumstances sounded. But something about the way her steely gaze met mine made me question myself. The way she spoke made something inside my chest, that I was unsure even existed, ache a little.

"Thank you." This was all I said. Something in her expression softened.

"Yeah. You're welcome, I guess." Then she shrugged and the softness was gone again.

Having covered what seemed like the most basic of information and both of us feeling no less confused, but completely exhausted by this inexplicable turn of events, Anna awkwardly announced that she was going to get in the shower. I scrambled around for an answer, but settled on nothing at all and merely smiled and nodded at her instead. She stared at me for a moment longer, still in complete disbelief, then shook her head, gathered her clothes and towel and disappeared into the bathroom.

She locked the door after her and I sat with my unusually light head in my hands for a while as I heard the shower turn on.

What the fuck must she think of me? What the fuck should *I* even think of me?
Sub-human. Ghastly. Corpse.
Ghost.

CHAPTER 2

ANNA

THE DAY RAN away as if time were foreign to us.

He had no choice but to linger in my room – this was apparent. We tried again and again to get him through the doorway, to absolutely no avail. The simple act of stepping through the frame was impossible to him, no matter which way we tried it. Windows were also not an option – the same thing seemed to happen. He just came up against some sort of barrier that was not really there. The same way that *he* wasn't really there.

Or shouldn't have been, but was.

I spent a lot of the day simply looking at him. Taking him in. I'm sure it made him uncomfortable, but nobody could say that it was unreasonable under the circumstances. I wonder if he had really seen *himself* yet, but decided not to ask, in case it came across as insensitive. He was obviously in deep discomfort and at times seemed completely overwhelmed by the situation. A few times throughout the day, he just sat and stared into space, or with his head in his hands, completely silent.

I couldn't even imagine what he was thinking and how scared he must've been. He didn't know who he *was*. Even the concept of it made my head spin.

In the evening light, he seemed much more real than he had during the day. The warmth from my lamps shone through him and the shape of him was much more distinguishable. He even cast a light shadow on the wall, in the right lighting. He was slightly shorter than other guys his age, (I didn't actually *know* how old he was, but from his mannerisms I guessed he couldn't have been much older than me, maybe 21 or 22) but the outline of his shoulders was broad and he was still quite a bit taller than me. It seemed that he could interact with his *own* body the way that any normal person could – throughout the day I watched him fiddle with his fingers and move his hair out of his eyes on more than one occasion. His slightly darker hair, still half-transparent, looked sort of feathery and parted in the middle, coming down to hang in front of his illusive grey eyes. The lines of his face were very straight and firm looking. I still couldn't quite believe that I could pass my hand through his entire form, if I applied enough force.

There was something gentle in his eyes. Despite their strange colour, they were not cold or lifeless at all. In fact, there was a childlike warmth about them, or some sort of vulnerability.

"Did you have classes today, that you were supposed to–"

"Uh, yeah, this morning, actually." I hadn't even thought about it before he'd mentioned it. I'd got the feeling recently that my tutors were beginning to give up on me a bit. The reassuring emails and encouraging comments had begun to fizzle out over the last week or so. But there was no need to tell him any of that. "It doesn't matter though."

He frowned, but eventually nodded.

"I mean," I shook my head a little, "I can catch up."

He was perched on my window ledge with his knees drawn up against his chest and his arms wrapped around them. He didn't look particularly comfortable, but I was glad that he wasn't sat too close to me. Observing him from a distance was okay for now, but I couldn't help but feel a chill run through me at the thought of touching him. I tried not to let it show.

"Your room has a lot of yellow." he said absent-mindedly, craning his head around to look at my walls.

He stood and walked around a bit, inspecting my posters and boards. I suddenly felt extremely exposed, with a complete stranger there in my private space, presumably feeling judgemental about the state that it was in. He paused for a moment in front of one of my notice-boards, looking at the pictures that I had pinned there. I saw his eyes pass over the ones of me and my friends at various parties, the one of my parents in front of the Eiffel Tower and smile to himself slightly.

My heart started to speed up as he settled on a photo of me and Charlie from the year before, standing in front of a Christmas tree. I hadn't had the heart to take it down. Every time I went near it, I suddenly became distracted with other things. Things that didn't make my hands shake, or make me feel light-headed and sick to the pit of my stomach. He stared at the picture, still and pensive. I hated that I didn't know what he was thinking, or what he was going to say–

"I like yellow," he said abruptly, abandoning the picture and turning to face me instead, "but I think I prefer green."

This made me frown. "You mean, you think you liked it, before…" I left it open ended.

He shrugged, but couldn't meet my eyes. "I don't remember. Maybe, though."

I couldn't think of a thing to say to him. There were so many unanswered questions and so much was infuriatingly unclear. The facts were this – he was obviously a ghost of some kind. As if wrapping my mind around that wasn't enough, he didn't know who he had been when he was alive, or why he was here.

I had never been a spiritual person. My mother was always the one more likely to want to celebrate the Winter Solstice, or tell stories of how she'd felt somebody's spirit lingering around her. I never believed her, even when I had been a small child. The rest of my family would only ever nod and give her kind smiles to humour her. My father would constantly joke that she had a screw loose, even when they'd been together happily. Back then, the joke had been affectionate, but nowadays it seemed more like an insult. But I couldn't even blame him, because part of me had always agreed with him. Of course, there was no such thing as ghosts, spirits, or phantoms. When people were gone, they were gone.

Except that evidently, they weren't.

"This is impossible." I mumbled. The statement hadn't needed any context. He merely nodded, sat back on my window ledge and watched me with careful eyes.

He moved the hair out of his eyes again. "Anna," A jolt went through me at the sound of my name in his mouth. I looked into his illusive eyes, imploring him.

But there was nothing to be said. His face was full of apologies that I knew he couldn't put into words. I just nodded to him, closed my eyes and tried not to let my breath catch in my throat.

No matter how much we both wanted it all to be a dream, it wasn't.

He didn't function the way that normal, living people did. He didn't need to eat, or drink, or sleep. For the next few mornings, I awoke with the feeling of him there, knowing before I even looked that he was still lingering in the room. On these mornings, he never spoke before I did – he always waited for me to say something first. Then, a look of relief would wash over him and he would smile in a shy sort of way and say something back to me.

One morning, we said nothing to each other for a full hour, because I just didn't have the energy. When I finally spoke, he turned from one of my books that lay open on my desk that he'd been reading, smiled as if to say 'thank you', and we began the day as if it hadn't happened. If nothing else, he was the most patient being I'd ever met.

Over time, he gradually asked more and more questions about my life, as if he was building a profile of me. When I asked him once why he inquired so much, he merely shrugged and said:

"You're the only person that I know."

It had made something sink inside of me. I wasn't sure he'd even intended it to sound as sad as it did.

I hadn't left the house since the day that he'd arrived. Once, when I'd gone to the kitchen to make myself some lunch, I came back to the room and he was sitting on my bed. He was resting his back against the headboard, his eyes closed. He looked uncomfortable and his form seemed rigid. He opened his eyes as soon as I walked through the doorway and heaved a sigh.

"What's wrong?" I said, confused.

He gave me an unconvincing smile. "Nothing."

It was obviously a lie. Something had happened to him whilst I was out of the room, but I couldn't even think what. He'd looked so distressed, I was *sure* of it. But he'd changed the subject quickly, and the moment got lost amongst the many other unanswered questions.

We talked, or sat quietly. I worked at my desk and he'd sit on my bed reading. I'd sleep and he'd wander about my room, his weightless feet not making a sound against my wooden floorboards. I'd play some music and he'd say 'I like this', or 'I'm not sure about this one', but he didn't recognise a single song. He *did* recognise some of the titles of the books I was reading, but when I asked if he'd ever read them, he'd shake his head. I knew that it didn't mean no, it just meant that he couldn't remember.

Sometimes we caught one another looking at each-other. After a while, once the fear of him had worn away slightly, I found it difficult to stop observing him – he was so different one minute to the next. Sometimes he was a dark shade of a man, blending with the shadows of the room like he was one himself. The next, he was warm and glowing, almost tangible. He could be light and eerie, more ghostlike than anything else, but then sometimes it was as if he were *real*, almost flesh and bone.

He was quiet and contemplative most of the time, but I could tell that he was desperately drinking everything in. Our situation was a delicate one. I tried my hardest not to lose my temper with him, or let any frustration show. He didn't have the answers that I wanted and I had to keep reminding myself that I didn't have the ones that he needed, either. I wanted to give them to him, but I just didn't know how.

HIM

Anna's life confused me.

I know that seems like such a ridiculous thing to say, considering the state of my *own* existence, but it did. From what I'd observed of Anna, aside from being slightly chaotic, (which I could hardly judge her for, she did have an amnesiac ghost unexpectedly lodging with her), she seemed like the sort of person that would be at the centre of everything. From the pictures on her walls, I could see that she had plenty of friends and seemed quite close with her parents. From a couple of photos that were pinned here and there, there also seemed to be some sort of boyfriend in the picture – her and him in front of the Christmas tree, them both underneath the same blanket in front of a beach fire. He looked a little older than her, maybe about 23 or 24 and was tall and a bit goofy looking, but with a charming smile in the photos. I could only assume that he was still a permanent fixture in her life, since the photos hadn't been taken down.

But she never mentioned anyone. Each time her phone rang, she muttered something like 'oh, fuck off' and turned it over, so she couldn't see who was calling. Nobody ever came by the house, not even just to check up on her. She was obviously completely capable of looking after herself – cooking, doing her work, cleaning up after herself (kind of) – but it seemed so strange to me that she chose to be so isolated.

So much of Anna seemed to be at odds with other parts of her. When she spoke, it often came across as harsh, but her face never seemed to reflect that same harshness. When she moved she was clumsy, quite often taking more than one object to the floor with her, but somehow she still seemed to be as weightless as I was and almost *graceful*. Quite often she would laugh completely humourlessly, but when she actually found something funny, her eyes would light up, but her voice would not follow. She could ramble tirelessly, but somehow none of her words lacked clarity.

I would often wonder what she thought of me, the ghoul that had invaded her space. She spent a lot of time just looking at me, like one might look at a puzzle that was missing the core pieces.

We had settled into a strange sort of rhythm with each-other, which I never would've expected to happen. I got the feeling that maybe Anna was used to spending a lot of time on her own, so I tried to let her lead and keep my distance a little too. I could tell that this was all overwhelming for her and that she needed some space. Instead, I read her books, watched the shows that she liked to watch, and when I could, I stole glances of her. I couldn't help it. She fascinated me.

But already I was keeping too much from her. But how could I tell her? How could I tell her, that every time she left the room it was as if the air was being sucked out of it and my body grew cold and weak? I'd tried to conceal it from her, but I knew that she already suspected. Anna was sharp and I could not get away with it for long. Why was it that every time that she left, I felt like I was... fading?

The walls of Anna's room were yellow, but somehow I felt like *she* was the one that radiated the warmth into it. And without her, all there was were four bleak walls, a barren bedroom and a ghost who might have been somebody, once.

ANNA

My mother called one evening.

The light was fading from the room and he was sat again at my desk, reading one of my books for my American Novel class – though he couldn't actually turn the pages without my help. The TV fizzed a little in the background because of bad signal and I wondered how he could concentrate on the words without complete silence. It would have driven me mad if I was trying to read.

I was apprehensive about him hearing me speak to my mum, because I didn't know what she might say and what he might overhear. A day or so earlier Sam had called, mainly just to check if there had been any parcels delivered for her while she'd been staying with her boyfriend, Jason. I hadn't had any problem putting her on speaker when we spoke, knowing that she would never mention Charlie, or ask about how any of my classes were going. Samantha had a tendency to avoid any subjects that she considered awkward – she was one of those people who couldn't bear any silences in conversation and would much rather keep things light and fluffy. After we'd spoke, I'd hung up the phone and glanced over to him to see him looking at me with an expression that I couldn't read.

But when mum had called, I found a reason to leave the room instead, hanging around in the hallway while we spoke.

"I just wanted to check in on you darling, I know we haven't spoken in a while." she said in her gentlest voice.

I laughed without much humour. "I know mum, I'm sorry. But the phone works both ways, you know."

I could feel her grimacing, even though I couldn't see her expression. "I'm sorry too, sweets. You know, it's just been so tough–"

"I know, mum. It's fine." I interrupted, already seeing how this conversation was going to go.

There was a short silence. "So, how are things?" she asked. "I've just been commissioned for another sculpture! For the library this time, actually, thank God. That place could use a bit of life injected into it, if you ask me. It's a lot of work to do and the deadline's pretty soon so I've been *very* busy, which is a bit of a shock to the system, you know? It's been a bit strange going back to work, I mean, since Charlie, but in a way I've found it's sort of helpful..."

I took the phone away from ear, let my hand fall to my side and rested my head back against the wall. The tinny sound of her voice rattled through me, even though I could barely make out what she was saying anymore. But I didn't want to hear her talk about Charlie, or anything else. I peered around the door-frame to check on him and saw that he was now watching the TV and had left his book open on the desk. I smiled a little, noting that I might have overestimated his powers of concentration.

I jumped when I realised that my mum was still prattling on down the phone and picked it up to listen again.

"...things with you, sweetheart? How are the classes going? Have you been spending lots of girl time with Sam and Hannah?"

I sighed gently. "Yeah, loads. We're having a film-night tonight, actually. Classes are fine too. Not much to report, really. I'm glad you're doing okay, though. I'm actually in the middle of an essay at the moment mum, can I give you a ring later in the week?" I said, trying not to let my voice sound strained.

She agreed, saying that she was (of course) extremely busy too and we'd catch up later on. I signed off by saying that I loved her and hung up with a deep breath to steady myself before I went back into the room.

He was looking at me again, apparently having abandoned the TV for good this time.

"Yes?" I inquired, maybe a little harshly, sitting back on top of my bed.

He cocked his head a little bit, looking like he was considering his words carefully before speaking.

"That was your mum?" He eventually asked, his eyes heavy with unspoken words.

I nodded silently. He pondered this for a moment.

"Tell me about her." he implored. The TV still fizzed in the background, but he seemed to barely notice it.

"She's an artist." I said, smiling in what I hoped was a convincing way. He smiled.

"And your dad? I mean, is he–"

"He's a carpenter, sort of. They're not together anymore. My parents, I mean." I replied.

"Right." he said, digesting. "And are they friendly, or was it difficult, you know–"

"They don't really see much of each other, to be honest. But when they do, they..." I paused for a moment, considering the right phrase. "They try."

I watched him take in everything that I had said, knowing that I hadn't given him much to go on at all. He swivelled in his chair slightly, wanting to face me head on.

"And what are they like?" he asked, leaning forward.

I stared at the wall through him, at the picture board behind him. I swept my eyes over the memories, trying to ignore the tightening feeling in my stomach.

"What do you mean?" I said at last. He laughed a little.

"I mean, *tell me about them.*" he said eagerly, then seemed to reconsider this approach. "Please?" he added, softer.

The room suddenly seemed a lot smaller than it had before. The walls were closing in on us and the lights were too bright and imposing, giving me a small ache in my temples. He sat in the chair, waiting patiently for me to answer. He watched me with his unreal face, carved from some ghostly marble, soft eyes rested on me. My breath was beginning to catch in my chest.

"Why?" I eventually croaked out. He seemed puzzled by my question, his brow furrowing slightly.

"Because..." he trailed off, looking away for a second. "I don't know, really. I mean, they're people in your life. The people you must know best. They must have hobbies, traits, I just want to know what they're like–"

"But *why*? Why does it matter?" I snapped back. He flinched a little at my tone, but did not shy away from answering.

"Because they must be important to you! But you never mention them! You never mention *anyone*, actually and I just want to know–"

"Me." I interrupted. "You want to know me?" I fixed him with a stare, but he did not flinch this time. He merely shrugged lightly.

"Yes." he replied simply. Then there was silence for a moment again.

"Because, what? Because you're stuck here? Because for some unknown reason you appeared in *my* room, not some other person?!" I was losing my patience now, the heat rising in my chest and feeling prickly at the base of my neck. "It could've been *anyone*. Why are you here questioning *me*, when I could be anyone? I don't *matter* to you–"

"Anna, that's not what I–"

"You think because you're here and not somewhere else that it has to *mean something*? That my family has to mean something? That my favourite colour has to mean something? That *I* have to mean something?!" I was breathing heavily now, rage shooting down my spine like a fever. But he was still, observing me.

"I just thought that, since I'm here..." he started

slowly, "Anna, I know that I haven't made life easy for you by being here. But *I* don't know anything, okay? And I'm just trying to get some information, because I–"

"So this is all just some kind of research to you? Try and figure me out and maybe you can figure out the rest?" I spat out, my head now reeling. I stood up and clenched my fists together at my sides, trying to relieve some of the anger.

"No, Anna. You're the only person that I can talk to..." he tried, but I was past the point of listening.

"You've got it wrong, okay? You shouldn't be trying to figure *me* out, alright? You should be trying to figure *you* out! *You're* the one who turned up here unannounced, all shimmery and out of the blue! *You're* the one who we need to be trying to research, so that you can actually–"

"What, Anna?" he asked, his voice harder than I'd ever heard it before. "So I can finally leave?! Trust me, I know that's what you really want."

"What I want, is to be *alone*, okay?! Not being constantly prodded and asked questions–"

"Anna, you know I can't leave."

"Yeah, well I can." I said, picking up my coat off the hook and putting it on and walking out the door. He called after me, but I was already out the back door and storming through the garden by the time I heard his voice.

HIM

She left, and I understood why. I knew that I was imposing on her, but I didn't know what else to do.

No matter how much space I tried to give her, it wasn't enough. I paced about her room while she was gone, going over the conversation again and again in my head, searching for something that I could have said to change the outcome. So that she wouldn't have gone. So I wouldn't be feeling like everything was being drained from me.

After a while, it was feeling laborious even to move around. A cold was trickling through me, from the base of my spine up towards my shoulders and I felt so weak that I had to sit down again. What was *happening* to me? I reached my arms out to grab the wall and pulled myself along it, trying to get to the bathroom, but my legs felt too heavy for my body and my head felt too light to focus. I managed to get myself in front of the mirror and held onto the rim of the sink for as long as my arms would allow, without simply falling through the basin. I tried to steady myself, then raised my head to look in the mirror.

What I saw made my head swim even more. Any colour that I'd had to my strange form an hour ago was almost entirely gone, so much so that I was beginning to blend into the harsh white of the bathroom walls behind me. Even as I was watching, it was getting harder and harder to make out the shape of me in the mirror. I was fading again. Only my eyes seemed to be the same as they had before she left, light and silvery, but still *there*.

"Shit." I whispered, bringing my hand up to touch my face, cringing when after a few moments my hand went straight through my ghostly skin.

I went to sit back on the window ledge again,

shivering when I sat down, unable to shrug off the chill any longer. After that, there was nothing I could do but wait. Wait for her to come back, knowing that I wouldn't blame her if she never did.

CHAPTER 3

ANNA

THE STREETS WERE seemingly empty, which I guess made sense considering that it was now late evening on a weekday and the area was hardly a social hub even on the weekends. The lamps struggled to light up the pavement, casting a half-hearted shadow on the concrete below me as I walked. There was a little light still left on the horizon, losing in its fight to overcome the dark as it settled in. Gently, the air whipped around me and I hugged my coat closer to avoid the chill.

When I'd come to the end of the road, I stared right, then left. Left would take me into town, but that felt like the last thing that I wanted at the moment. Right would take me further into the suburbs, where I knew there was a park and a small field that the local football team sometimes used to practice. Opting for silence rather than the daunting prospect of people, I veered right. I walked quickly, apparently made faster with rage spurring me on and even the moon seemed to hide away from my wrath behind the clouds, peeking its head out every now and then to check if the coast was clear.

When I arrived at the field, I sat on the bench alone for a while and let my thoughts finally wash over me, unable to hold them back much longer. The playing field was utterly deserted, so nobody was there to see the water pool in my eyes, then make tracks down my cheeks. Nobody was there to hear me shout in frustration, swearing until my throat felt raw and sore and I could no longer project my voice. Nobody was there to stop me when I swung my balled-up fists against the bench beneath me. The hollow feeling in my stomach was growing again and something was gnawing at the insides of me. But nobody was there.

When all was said and done, the silence settled around me like a blanket that I had assumed would be comforting, but was not. It was heavy and weighed down on my chest and I wanted to go home.

I wanted someone to be there.

HIM

It was like slipping into sleep in a lake of still, cold water. Your movements are slow, laboured. Your head is clouded and heavy. And you are *so* cold.

I hardly heard her come into the room when she did. I was descending to somewhere else. I was far away from myself, or at least from the shell that was sat on Anna's window ledge. I was sinking below. I was nearly gone.

Her figure blurred as it came towards me in urgency, all cloudy movements that seemed to overlap with each other. I could see her ivory skin as her face came level with mine. I could see her big green eyes, wide and filled with fear. I tried to speak, but nothing came.

ANNA

By the time I'd gotten back into the room, he was barely there.

It took me some time to even find him. When I

walked into the room, I couldn't see him anywhere. It took me a few moments of searching to actually *see* him, there again, crumpled against my window, his outline barely visible. Before I could even register my movements, I was kneeling over by him, beginning to hyperventilate.

"Hey. What the hell is happening?!" I spoke loudly, in case he couldn't hear me.

His frame was more fragile than it had been before. There was no colour to him at all, it was like he was a mirage, or a wisp of smoke in the shape of a man. He was fading fast, his form flickering in and out of the light, barely discernible now. He had his head back against the wall, his eyes opening and closing tiredly.

"Hey!" I said, inching closer to him to inspect him further, having to squint to make him out properly. "I can't – I mean – I don't know what to do, what should I do?!"

But it was no use, he was completely unresponsive, like he was drifting in and out of consciousness and couldn't even hear me. I could feel panic rising in me and felt completely helpless. But there must be *something*. I leaned forward so that there were only centimetres between us.

"Just *talk* to me!" I heard the words tumbling out of me, dripping with desperation. "Please, I don't know how to help," I reached out instinctively to grab his arm, knowing that my hand would only be reaching out into the empty space where he should be.

And I touched him.

I felt a jolt of electricity run up my arm with the shock of it – *I could feel him*. My hand rested on his arm as though he were human, as though he were *solid*. As though he were alive. I could feel his skin against mine, soft like silk but *there*, and when I gripped harder my hand did not pass through him.

My head was beginning to feel light as I stumbled back a little, still holding on to him. But by some miracle he was stirring again, his head rolling back a little against the wall and sighing. Everything inside me jolted a little and I stroked a line up and down his arm to try and get his attention. And his *colour* was coming back. He was there again, a faint and delicate version of his form, but there nonetheless, more and more tangible to my eyes by the second. *He was coming back.*

I heaved a breathy laugh, relief washing over me. I didn't let go of his arm, I merely sat on the floor beneath him, looking quietly at him as he returned to himself. I could make out more and more of him now – the slight creases by the sides of his eyes, the slant to his chin, even the delicate outlines of his eyelashes. Then his eyes opened. He searched my face, then cast his clouded eyes down to look at my hand, now rested on his wrist. A small smile played on his lips as he closed his eyes and rested his head back against the wall.

"You're back." He said softly. His words stayed in my head like he had planted them there.

"I can…" I whispered quietly, "I can feel you." The words caught in my throat, though I did not know why.

He opened his eyes again, watching me carefully. Trying to detect panic in my eyes. I don't know what he saw there, but he raised his other hand. After a moment's consideration, I raised mine too, and slowly we pressed our palms flat against the other's.

He waited for a few moments, for his hand to press through mine and fall through to the other side. But the moment did not come.

HIM

I could touch her.

"How?" She managed to murmur, her eyes dark and curious, marvelling at our hands still held together.

I shook my head lightly. "I don't… I don't know." I heaved out a sigh that my body did not need.

There they were, our hands. Hers, palm warm but fingertips cold, pressed against mine. Mine, translucent and eerie, *pressed against hers.* Until she looked up at me and drew her hand back steadily, letting it fall to her side.

How much have I scared her? How unequipped is she to process this information? My gaze flicked rapidly about her face, seeking some sign as to what was going on behind her eyes. She held my gaze steady for a few moments, unbearably quiet. Her other hand was still resting on my wrist.

"Anna…" I started, but she shook her head in reply. She looked away from me for a moment, staring down at her lap. "Anna, if this is too much–"

"I'm so sorry." She interrupted in a whisper, and when she raised her head I was shocked to see her green eyes full of sincerity. There was no guard up at all. She was there in front of me, completely earnest. There was a hint of red to her cheeks and the lines of her face seemed softened somehow. The impulse to reach out and brush a stray hair from her face nearly overwhelmed me, so much so that I had to take a breath to settle myself.

"I shouldn't have," She began, but it was my turn to talk.

"Anna, I shouldn't be here." I said gently, trying to get her to look into my eyes. She held my gaze and listened intently. "I shouldn't be in your space, in your life. I should be somewhere else entirely. I think we both know that. But I *am* here, with you." I sighed. "I came here with no warning and I'm sorry about that. You didn't ask for this and I'm sorry about that, too. You were right when you said it could have been anyone. But I'm not… I'm not sorry that it's you." I paused. "Not at all."

She was still for a minute and my words hung between us in the silence. Her eyes flitted down to look at her hand, still resting on my wrist.

"Me neither." she said in a low voice. And the whole world came back into focus

Feeling more like myself, whoever or whatever that might be, Anna told me to sit on her bed while she laid her head back on her pillow, digesting everything that had happened. She closed her eyes for a moment, her dark hair splayed all over the cream bedspread. Her cheeks still looked flushed, though whether it was from the cold outside or from the adrenaline, I wasn't sure. I cast my eyes over her for a second while she rested. With all the commotion, I hadn't noticed that she had discarded her jacket, but now saw that she was wearing a simple grey t-shirt with thin straps and black leggings and fluffy socks of different colours on her feet. One yellow, one pink. I smiled slightly. The act of wearing odd socks was somehow so unapologetically *Anna.* Her eyelashes fluttered slightly and she opened her eyes.

"What?" she mumbled quietly, a touch of annoyance in her tone.

"Mm?" I replied. She nodded towards me, gesturing at my smile.

"What's that face for?" she asked. I felt my smile widen, but shook my head dismissively.

"Nothing, nothing." I said, looking away for a moment in an attempt to compose myself.

The room was dark getting really dark now, and I walked over to Anna's desk to try to turn the lamp on for some light. Leaning down, I paused for a moment with my hand hovering over the lamp switch, then tried gently to press down on it. The bulb flickered for a moment under the lampshade, but my fingers pushed through it before I could get it on and we were shrouded in darkness again. I huffed in frustration and hung my head for a moment.

Anna, watching me, swung her legs over the side of the bed and got up to come over to me. She turned on the lamp with ease, casting light over her desk and walls. The picture board hanging above the desk was visible and Anna's friends stared out at me with smiles on their faces. I focused again on the picture of her and the charming-faced guy, on the beach, laughing together. I frowned and glanced at her, but she was looking at another picture.

A man with a slightly unruly dark beard and kind, dark eyes stood tall over a dainty looking woman in an oversized red jumper – she had a huge grin on her face. Anna's gaze was fixed on the picture.

"That's them." she said, raising her hand and putting her finger on the picture, in the gap between the two smiling faces. "My mum and dad."

I nodded, not taking my eyes from her. "I assumed, yeah."

She kept her finger there for a moment, rubbing the picture slightly as if she was trying to get some feeling from it. Then she dropped her hand, sighed and went back to lie on the bed. But this time, she kept her eyes open, staring at the mouldings on the ceiling.

"She's kind of exhausting, my mum," she said into the space. I walked slowly back to the bed and perched upon it, not wanting to disturb her train of thought. "I mean, she's always been like that. She's got this energy, this kind of... spirit about her, I guess. You never know what she's going to do one minute to the next. She's sort of intense and sometimes it can be in a really great way. But then..."

"Sometimes, it's not." I finished for her. She looked over to me for a second, then nodded.

"I don't think it ever even really bothered my dad, though. I think he might have even liked that about her, once. He's always been a bit regimented, hard to get out of a routine. So I think when she came along, all carefree and wherever-the-wind-takes-us kind of thing, they just... fit." She started fiddling with a loose strand of cotton from the quilt, ravelling and unravelling it around her fingertip. "You know, the way some people do."

I watched her play with the thread, wrapping it so hard around her finger that it looked like it might hurt.

"So, what happened?"

She didn't look up from the thread, but shrugged. "Something pushed them apart."

Something. The same something that had her calling out in the dark.

I paused for a moment, wanting to proceed carefully. I knew that it was a privilege to have gotten this far and I was wary of her putting up her walls again. Clearly they could go up a lot faster than they could be broken down.

"And it pushed you away from them, too." I said, and her green eyes glanced up at me for a second, then went back to the loose thread around her finger.

"Maybe," she said quietly, "but I think I might have been the one who did the pushing there."

She smiled slightly, but her eyes stayed low. Her fingers were working quickly, ravelling and unravelling. Without even thinking, I reached out and put my hand over hers, which then fell still. She looked up at me then, her vast eyes reaching out to mine. I could feel her skin underneath my fingers, solid and unbelievable. I glanced down at our hands and resisted the urge to stroke her wrist with my thumb.

"You're thinking so much that you aren't saying." she said. I laughed ironically and nodded, because she had no idea how right she was.

I *wanted* to ask her what had hurt her so much. I

wanted to say that whatever it was, she shouldn't be alone. I wanted to say that her parents shouldn't have let her push them away. That her friends should be here. That her boyfriend should come and visit. I wanted to say that she was the last person in the world who should ever be in pain. I wanted to say that everything would be okay, even though I was starting to get the feeling that that wasn't at all the truth. And God, I wanted to stroke her wrist with my thumb.

"I just hate that you're hurting." I said simply, avoiding her gaze.

"But, you don't even know me. Not really." she said bluntly.

I laughed again. "Bloody right. You're a complete mystery to me." I said with a smile.

By some miracle, she smiled back, then nudged my hand with hers. "Ironic, coming from you."

I grinned at her, then shrugged.

"Yeah, we're a right pair." I nodded. I moved my fingers over hers, testing the waters a little. Without looking at me, she grabbed one of my fingers with hers and held onto it. We looked at each other.

"Anna, why can we touch?" I asked, knowing that she had no answer. She shook her head, looking back to our hands together on the bed.

"I don't know." she said.

I spoke the words silently in my head. *Maybe we just... fit.*

While Anna slept that night, exhausted from all the strange happenings of the evening, still wearing her odd socks, I sat at her window and contemplated everything that I thought I knew.

What would have happened, had Anna not come back into the room when she did? If she hadn't touched me and the life hadn't flowed back into my half-body the way that it had? Where would I be now? Would I even be anything? I'd been slipping *somewhere* before she'd brought me back.

I glanced over to her, all wrapped up in her sheets and breathing steadily in the darkness. There was a peace to her then that was never there when she was awake. A peace that I wished could stay with her. But I was there and things with her family were fucked up and her head was too full of dark thoughts that she never shared for the peace to linger.

She sighed gently then, as if she knew that my worries were with her. Against all my better judgement, I stood and walked over to her bedside, my body ignoring my head's protests. I kneeled next to her on the floor, watching her eyelids as they fluttered slightly in sleep. For a moment, there was nothing but the sound of her light breathing that filled the room. Everything else was still and nothing outside of this room even existed. Before I knew what I was doing, I raised my hand and moved a stray hair out of her face, tucking it behind her ear. I revelled in how simple it all was, how human it felt to touch her.

With my touch, she stirred gently, humming soft in her stupor. Her eyelids fluttered open and I froze completely, caught in her gaze. Unable to speak or even move, I could do nothing but smile at her sleep-filled eyes. She watched me for a moment.

"Hi." she whispered quietly. Everything inside me

felt like it was breaking when I felt her breath fan my face.

"Hi." I said back, trying to keep my voice steady.

She didn't smile, or say anything after that. She didn't ask why I was there, kneeling beside her bed, only inches away from her resting body. She merely reached out for my hand and tucked it beneath hers on the mattress and was falling back to sleep again, seemingly unaware of how the feeling of her skin against mine was making my breath hitch in my chest.

Peace settled over her again. My mind turned over a hundred times, reeling over the feeling of it all. How had she done that? With one simple gesture, she'd said everything that needed to be said.

I'm glad you're here. I'm here with you, too.

I sighed heavily, hanging my head, my hand still resting underneath hers as she slept.

All of this was going to hurt, I realised in that moment. Every single moment was going to hurt.

ANNA

Everything moved slowly the next morning, as if we were in some kind of dream. We both knew that something had happened in the night. Some sort of acceptance had washed silently over us both and neither of us had to speak it out loud for it to be known.

I'm glad you're here. I'm here with you, too.

"What's on the agenda for today?" he asked, while I stood in my bathroom, tying my hair up and away from my face. I shrugged.

"Not sure, really. Staying in again, I guess, since you

can't be here without me." I chuckled, glancing over to where he sat on my bed.

He laughed too, swinging his legs over the edge of the bed and walking over to the doorway, testing his boundaries again. He lifted his palms up against the frame again, pressing and pressing, to no avail. Something still pushed back and he made a sound of annoyance at the back of his throat.

"Forget it, Rapunzel. You're stuck in this tower. Maybe you can let your hair down for me, next time I go to the shops." I teased, grinning at him.

He slumped his illusory body down at my desk, grumbling.

"So emasculating." He shook his head in mock shame. I laughed in spite of myself.

The sunlight was glowing through him today, lighting him up like a hologram. He ran his hands through his hair distractedly. My eyes lingered on his slender hands for a moment too long, remembering the feeling of his fingers underneath my own as I slept, the look in his eyes when I had woken in the night. He caught me looking at him and smiled, curious. Trying to read me. I thought about touching him again.

"What?" he said.

"I have an idea." I said, cocking my head to the side slightly. His curiosity grew and he raised his eyebrows expectantly.

"We can touch, right?" I said animatedly, walking towards him quickly and grabbing his hand from his lap. He was surprised at my touch but didn't recoil, he merely laced his fingers through mine.

"Seems that way." he murmured, eyes fixed on our

hands together. He breathed out slowly, then looked up to me.

"So, what if..." I trailed off, shaking my head. I tugged at his hand, pulling him out of the chair until he was stood next to me, body only inches from mine. Then I started dragging him towards the doorway and he started shaking his head at me, frowning.

"Anna, I can't–" he started, but I cut him off.

"Let's just try, because if we're touching–"

But he was still shaking his head, looking defeated. "Anna, I'm just gonna bounce back when you go through." He laughed humourlessly.

But I was already at the doorway, determined. I moved through into the hallway, arm outstretched, hand still holding his through the gap in the wall. I smiled at him encouragingly.

"Come through." I said, nodding at him. He sighed, twisting his hand in mine. Then he moved forward tentatively.

And walked through the doorway.

His eyes widened as he stood next to me and I started laughing gleefully. He looked frantically between our hands, still clasped together tightly, then up to my face, then back to the doorway.

Then he started laughing breathlessly, completely incredulous.

"Well that changes things a bit." he laughed, looking down at me. "How the hell did you know that was going to work?!"

I shrugged. "Honestly, I didn't. It was just a guess. Mad, right?" I laughed and he whipped his head around, taking in the new surroundings.

"Paradigm shifting." he muttered. He fixed his eyes on the doorway again, peering into my bedroom. "I'm not stuck anymore."

I laughed. "Just with me, by the looks of it." I started to unravel our hands, but he held mine tightly, unaware. He glanced down to me again, eyes full of something I couldn't recognise.

"Could be worse." he muttered, looking away quickly. "God, this is all so fucking weird."

"Yeah, I know. I didn't really think it would work but–" He dropped my hand suddenly and wandered off to the kitchen.

I laughed, following him through. It was so strange seeing him there, ghostly and light against the harsh white of the tiles, leaning against the kitchen cabinets. His head swivelled around frantically as he walked, drinking in everything he could. He turned to face me, grinning.

"Anna, *I'm in the kitchen!*"

Something lurched inside me at the sight of him so happy, so full of wonder. I couldn't hold back a laugh.

"Can we go outside?" he said suddenly. "Let's go for a walk, please."

"What, where everyone can see you? You must be mental." I replied in disbelief. He just shrugged.

"We can just go somewhere private, or quiet! There must be somewhere where hardly anyone goes around here? What's the worst that could happen?" he said nonchalantly, peering out of the window into the small garden. I felt like my jaw was about to drop off.

"You mean, other than my neighbours seeing me walking around with a literal *ghost?*"

"What, so I can leave the room, but now I have to stay stuck in the house forever? I thought I just got out of the Rapunzel state!" He smiled.

"I literally cannot believe what I'm hearing," I replied, unable to stop the shock from underlying my words, "Have you forgotten that you are *transparent?* Like, *see-through?*" But my words weren't even touching him, I could already see the cogs whirring in his head, formulating a completely reckless and nonsensical plan. "What the hell am I supposed to say if somebody sees you?! 'Don't worry, me and Casper have just been stuck inside for a few days and fancied a *Saturday stroll–*'"

"Can you drive?" he interrupted, eyes wide and full of hope.

I sighed. "Yeah, my car's parked out the back. But we're not–"

He strode up to me then, grabbing my hands in his, sending a jolt through me, right to the base of my spine. My words faltered when he looked down at me, warm eyes melting into mine. He ran his thumbs gently over my knuckles.

"Anna, the most I've seen of the outside is from your bedroom window." he mumbled quietly, his voice full of sincerity. "I can't remember what the wind looks like when it blows through the trees. I want to see it."

I wrinkled my nose. "You know, technically you can't see the wind blowing through the trees. That's the whole point of wind–"

He threw his head back and made a sound of frustration, which made me laugh. Then his eyes were back on mine.

"Anna!" He was grinning, all warmth and childish excitement. "Please?"

I sighed, all but defeated. I dropped my hands from his and leaned over to the counter to grab my car keys.

"I swear, if we see anyone..."

But he was practically skipping towards the back door.

CHAPTER 4

HIM

"The good news is that I don't have to wear a seatbelt." I said, when she pulls out of the parking space with a look of concentration fixed on her face.

"Hmm? Why not?" Anna muttered in reply, distracted.

"Well, I'm not exactly about to break any bones, am I?" I teased, grinning over at her. "If anything happens, I'm going straight through the windshield, no damage. Safe as anything."

She laughed at this, then looked confused. Her eyebrows came together in a way that was undeniably cute.

"Wait, do you even *have* bones?" she half-laughed. Her road disappeared behind us as we took a right turn.

"I mean, you'd hope so. At one point." I raised my hand in front of me, moving it slowly across my eyeline. The dashboard of Anna's car was visible through the outline of my palm.

Anna snorted humourlessly, eyes flicking towards me and my ghostly hand for a moment before returning to the road ahead.

"I feel like I've been dreaming for days." she muttered quietly. I was glad to hear that there was no malice behind her words.

I shook my head lightly, then turned to watch the

peaks of trees and houses speed by as we passed them.

"Me too." I replied quietly. *Thank God I'm not.*

There were no other cars parked around. It would have been easy to believe that we were miles away from civilisation, or any other people, when in reality the road we'd turned off was only a few minutes away. Anna had made me duck down in my seat every time we had passed someone whilst driving. It made me laugh uncontrollably, seeing her so overcome with stress about it all.

After all, what was anyone going to think, had they seen me for only a few moments? Some truths aren't ready to be spoken, let alone accepted.

Anna looked completely ridiculous as she stepped out of the car, dressed in a colossal puffy coat, dark green like her eyes. It enveloped her entirely, so she was almost just a pair of big eyes peeking above a mountain of material. Her cheeks were already flushed from the cold, tinted pink against the usual paleness of her skin. I couldn't help but stare as she zipped up her coat while I was still sat in my seat.

"What?" she said, defensive under my gaze. I shook my head slowly, trying not to laugh.

"Anna, that coat…" I started, unable to muster the right words.

"I run cold!" she replied snappily, shutting the car door and walking around to my side.

"*Nobody* runs *that* cold!" I said through the open window. She rolled her eyes, but there was a hint of warmth in her expression still.

"You wanna stay in the car, or…?" she said, arms

folded against her chest as she stood outside of my car door.

I was unable to stop myself from grinning at her stood there, so small and cloaked in her huge coat, giving off so much attitude.

"Sorry, sorry." I said, holding up my hands as a sign of defeat. Her smile was faint but genuine and she opened the door for me.

The woods were dense and from the small spot where Anna had parked the car, it took us only moments of walking to have lost sight of it. Pine trees towered over us both from every direction, completely dwarfing us in comparison. Groups of small black birds clung to the higher branches with their feet, swaying when the wind rushed through the trees. For the first few minutes we followed a path through the green, but after a while the path disappeared and we carried on without direction. Anna walked ahead of me and I tuned my ears to listen to the sounds that she made as she moved. The crunch of dead leaves underneath the weight of her steps. The sound of her breath hitching when she considered which way to go next.

Silently, I followed on behind her, like a shadow.

After a while, she fell back into step with me. She walked with her eyes lowered, a hundred cogs working in her mind.

"You were someone." she said quietly, like she had spoken the words already in her head before saying them aloud. Like they were carefully considered. "Before this."

She looked over to me, but I couldn't meet her eyes. So I raised my eyes to the treetops, watching the birds clutch onto the dead twigs of the pines.

"I suppose so." I said slowly.

"You didn't come from *nowhere*. You were someone, you came from somewhere."

I nodded, facing her now. Her eyes were gentle, considerate. The stray hairs that had escaped from her hair-tie flew wildly around her face.

"From somewhere, yeah. I just don't know where."

She nodded slowly, like she was considering what I'd said. Her eyes lowered to the ground again.

"You had a name. And a family." Her voice was barely above a whisper.

I was quiet for a moment, unable to speak.

"God, I really hope there isn't a dog out there somewhere, waiting for me to come home." I said with some humour, glancing down to see her reaction.

Her eyes widened in horror and her mouth formed a small 'o'. I tried to resist the urge to laugh.

"Why would you even *say* something like that?!" Her voice was grave and hurt and I let out a small huff of laughter.

She sighed deeply, shaking her head and wrapping her enormous coat around her, trying to keep the warmth in.

"What about… Jack?" she suggested suddenly, looking up at me again quizzically. I frowned at her, shaking my head.

"Doesn't ring a bell." I said honestly. She laughed a little.

"Yeah, you don't really look like a Jack."

She stopped in her tracks suddenly and stepped in front of me, blocking my path. She fixed me with her gaze, looking at me with everything she had. Looking *through* me, frowning.

"Ben?" she inquired. "No, Harry!" she grinned.

We both knew it was pointless to speculate. Whatever my name had been, it was a mystery to me now. But I couldn't resist the way her face was screwed up in concentration, trying to think of other options. For a moment, she was light. And I'd do anything for her to keep that feeling.

"Come on!" I said, "It's got to be something cool! Like… Jet."

She burst out laughing at this, clutching at her ribs and nearly doubling over.

"*What?* I could definitely pull off Jet!" I said, feigning offence. She gathered herself slightly, looking up at me through eyelashes that were slightly damp from laughter.

"No way." She shook her head. "Norman, maybe."

We smiled at each other for a moment, quiet and contemplative. The light was starting to fade from the sky and I knew that we should be turning back soon. But neither of us spoke. The sun dwindled behind the pines and cast streaks of warm light over Anna's face, catching the green of her eyes and dousing them in honey. For a moment, everything stilled around us. The birds stopped swaying in the branches. The stray hairs that framed her porcelain face fell still.

She cast her eyes over my form, transformed in the light of the setting sun. The beams of light shone through me, pooling warmth on the ground beneath me. I wondered what I looked like, to her.

"Does it hurt?" she asked, her voice *so* gentle.

I considered her question for a moment, bringing my hand up for the hundredth time, peering through it in wonder.

"No. I can't feel things in that way, I don't think anything would hurt–" I started to explain, but she shook her head and closed her eyes for a moment.

Then she took a step towards me and touched my arm lightly. Then, gently, she moved her hand to rest on the middle of my chest. I could feel the warmth from her palm soaking through me, sending *life* through me. I tried to keep my gaze steady as she looked into me.

"I mean, does it *hurt?*"

Her question felt as though it sent shockwaves through me. Like the earth shifted beneath my feet. For a moment, I felt like I might shatter entirely and I had to take a breath to steady myself.

I think of her calling out in the night, eyes red and swollen from tears. I think of her voice, strained and tired as she speaks to her mother on the phone. I think of her, ravelling and unravelling a loose thread around her finger, over and over.

I think of her pain and swallow my own.

"Not really." I smiled down at her, trying not to let sadness tinge my voice. I placed my hand over hers. "The beauty in not remembering, I guess. I don't *miss* anything. I don't even know what I'm supposed to miss."

She took her hand away then and I thought I could feel a coldness where we'd once touched. With her arms stretched wide open, she took a couple of steps back from me.

"What about all of this?"

I looked around for a moment. Pinks and oranges of all hues had invaded the sky and the trees were casting long spindly shadows on the ground. Something intangible inside me ached. But I could feel her gaze on me, so I turned back to her, shrugging.

"I have a version of this, at least." I said. *And I have you.*

She smiled wryly and shook her head, avoiding my eyes. But she dropped it, falling back into step with me again, her arm bumping mine every so often.

"Let's go back." I said. "It's about to get cold."

She nodded and we turned back towards the faint sounds of the road.

ANNA

We walked in comfortable quiet for a while, the only sound that broke the silence being one of us pointing out something of note to the other. We were only a few minutes from the parking spot now, which was good because the fading light was making it harder to see and I was starting to get worried that we might actually lose the car. I was trying to catch sight of the path back to the car, lost in thought, when I heard him speak my name.

"Earth to Anna!" he laughed.

"Sorry, what?"

"You didn't hear me! I said, 'look, a dog!'" He pointed and a hundred yards or so away was a black Labrador, bounding around the tree trunks.

"Aw!" I said, grinning.

But a look of concern had dawned rapidly on his

face and his silver eyes had widened. I grabbed his arm, but he was whipping his head around frantically, looking for something.

"What–"

"Uh, this guy's owner is going to be around somewhere." he interrupted.

Shit. I joined him in searching, but no matter how much we squinted, we couldn't see anyone. The dog approached us joyfully, then ran in between our legs, bouncing off behind us.

"You alright, love?" Came an unfamiliar voice from behind us, freezing us in our tracks.

Shit.

Slowly, staring at each other, we turned around to face the stranger.

He stood only a few steps from the two of us – a rather small, stout man, dressed in what I could only imagine was fishing gear, with a rod slung over his shoulder. The Labrador was settled at the man's feet, panting happily. The man's face was kind, his head cocked to the side slightly, looking at me with curious eyes.

I could feel my breath speeding up with each second that passed, but I tried to be the picture of calm, unfazed. Next to me, he slowly slid his hand down my arm, until it was wrapped gently around my wrist, holding it. He was completely silent.

I need to speak. "Uh, yeah, sorry. You just, made me jump. I didn't realise anyone else was out here." I said, my voice wavering slightly at the beginning.

"Sorry, love. Me and Jumbles are just on the way back to the car." The man replied, leaning down to scratch behind the dog's ears.

"Right, yeah."

I had literally no idea what to say. *Why* wasn't he mentioning the transparent guy next to me?! Why wasn't he even *looking* at him? He just had his concerned eyes fixed on *me!*

"Uh, well, you should be getting on, little lady." He gestured towards the tops of the trees with his hand. "S'getting dark. You shouldn't be out here by yourself, you know?"

What?!

Next to me, he snapped his head to look at me and it took absolutely all of my willpower not to do the same. Words floated around in my mind aimlessly and I grabbed at a few of them at random.

"Uh yeah, thanks. I'm nearly at my car." I ground out, trying my best to ignore the transparent guy next to me, who was wildly twisting his head to look between me, then the man in front of us.

The fisherman frowned at me, but nodded and eventually moved along, calling his dog after him.

"Don't say anything 'till we're back in the car." I whispered and we started walking hastily towards the car, eyes still fixed upon the retreating figure of the man and his dog.

Once we were back on the road, heat blasting through the vents in the car, we started theorising.

"What the *fuck* was that about?" I said, crossing lanes. Next to me, he shook his head, quiet.

"Anna, he couldn't–"

"*Nope.*" I declared loudly, shaking my head firmly.

"Don't even start–"

"Anna." He tried again, putting more force behind his voice.

I didn't turn my head away from the road. "It was dark." I said, steadily.

"He thought you were on your own, Anna!" He'd turned his entire body towards me, imploring me.

"Yeah, because it was dark! You're hardly visible when it's dark." My voice broke towards the end of my sentence, I wasn't making a compelling argument.

"He was stood four feet away from us! And the sun hasn't even set properly yet!" he exclaimed, gesturing out the window with his illusory arm. Oranges and reds still streamed through the window.

I shook my head firmly, unwilling to budge.

"Anna," he tried, this time more softly, "*that guy could not see me. He just saw you.*"

He reached out to touch me then, gently stroking a line back and forth on my forearm. I braved a glance towards him, wanting to know what his eyes were saying. They swept over me, full of concern and sincerity.

I shook my head. "I know." I heaved a sigh. "*I know, but how?*"

The silence that filled the expanse of the car was deafening. He tried to roll down his window by pressing down on the button, but his translucent hand merely pushed straight through it. I looked over to him and this time he held my gaze, reaching a hand out to tuck a stray hair away safely from my face.

He shook his head absentmindedly. He seemed to drift in and out of himself for a moment, becoming completely unreadable.

"Hey?" I asked, trying to catch his eyeline.

His silver eyes snapped towards me, but only for a moment. I threw glances at him whilst driving. He seemed irritable, running his hands through his faintly dark hair and pressing his fingertips to the bridge of his nose.

"What..." I started, unsure of where the sentence would even end up, "what are you thinking?"

But he just shook his head in the silence, watching the cars pass by us as we drove through the twilight.

He was lost in his thoughts – this much was obvious. What was killing me was that he wouldn't let me in on them.

He swept silently through the house and into my bedroom as soon as we got through the front door. I followed him down the hallway and watched him lie down on my bed with a deep sigh, letting his hands run over his ghostly face as though it might relieve whatever stress he was feeling.

I moved to the bedside, discarding my coat and dropping it at my feet. I stood over him for a minute, considering what to say. For a moment, I toyed with the idea of just leaving him there, offering him some space. But seeing him there, lying on my chequered bedspread, a million thoughts running through his troubled mind – I found that I couldn't.

"Will you just..." I began to say, then cleared my throat and tried again. "Please, talk to me."

He sat bolt upright suddenly, staring straight ahead blankly, not looking at me.

"And say what, exactly? What do you want me to say?" he said, his voice heavy with exhaustion.

I flinched a little at his tone, then collected my thoughts enough to speak.

"Anything." I said simply.

He turned to face me; eyes empty of their usual warmth.

"I can't shed light on *any* of this, Anna. I don't know what to say."

I sighed, feeling anxiety and irritation rise in my chest. I walked around the bed to him, kneeling in front of where he was sat.

"Try." I said, ducking my head so I could hold his gaze again.

He puffed out a sigh. "I'm just," He began shaking his head again, defeatedly. "I'm fucking all this up."

I frowned at him. "Fucking what up?" I asked, confused.

"All of this!" He opened his arms and held them that way, gesturing towards the open room. "This! You! Being here!"

I shook my head, bewildered. "I don't get it."

"Ugh." he replied, standing up suddenly and starting to pace back and forth at the foot of the bed. "Of course, of course you don't get it."

I reeled back a little at his reply. "*Explain* it to me then."

He shook his head as he paced and when he spoke his voice was louder, *sharper* than I'd ever heard it before.

"I'm just, here. And I'm *supposed* to be – I mean, shit. I *think* I'm supposed to be..." But he trailed off, leaving me even more confused than ever.

I was probably looking up at him like he was a madman. But I was completely at a loss as to what was happening.

"Uh, okay." I said, scratching my head. "That was, like, *nearly* a proper sentence."

He whipped his head around to look at me, stopped pacing and rooted himself to the floor.

"I just, I thought that there must be a reason that I was *here*." His voice had softened a little now and he was looking down at me with desperation. "But Anna, me being here, it's not doing anything except driving us both crazy!"

His words felt like a swipe at my chest, though I wasn't entirely sure why.

"That's not... true." I said quietly.

He barked out a humourless laugh, looking at me with wild eyes. The lamp behind him lit his strange form from behind, catching his outline in the light.

"No?" He countered, his voice wavering, "So, you haven't felt like you're losing it, ever since I arrived? Like you're literally losing your mind?! *I saw it*, Anna. In the car. I saw your face." He shook his head maniacally, then ran his hands through his hair again. "You can't lie, okay? Every time you feel like you're getting a handle on this... I don't even know, our *situation*, something else happens to make you completely question your sanity! And trust me, I'm with you there, okay? I get it. You're not alone there."

He started pacing again and I was quiet for a moment, processing all that he'd said.

"I'm not a kid, you know." I replied steadily. "I can

handle it. I thought that was obvious, I mean, after last night–"

"Right, exactly! Last night!" He interrupted, bringing his transparent hand to gesture towards me. "You couldn't handle it last night! And why should you? I mean, you're the *only* person in the world that has shown me any sort of decency, or, like... kindness. You let me lurk about in *your* room. You bring me back from whatever fucked up precipice I was on last night."

He was rambling and had to take a breath to steady himself. I was quiet, just listening to his outpour.

"But it just keeps getting more *confusing*. More *questions*. More *doubts* and you're sad and confused and – Shit. I mean, you had a *life*. You should be at university, doing your classes and–"

I can't help but scoff at this, which turns out to be the absolute worst possible reaction. He stared at me with wide eyes.

"Don't just scoff, like it's nothing! You had *something*, a life–"

Something inside me snapped. I couldn't hold back my words any longer.

"Alright, *enough!*" I shouted at him and he stepped back a little, taken aback at my anger. "Enough, okay? Enough acting like you have a fucking *clue* what you're talking about. Because you don't. You want to know what life was like before you got here?" I was reeling now, fire burning deep in my chest, fuelling my words.

He took a step towards me, cautiously. "Anna, I–"

"How about I give an overview? Just give you the

highlights." I snapped. "All fine for the first year of University, nothing really interesting to report." I started, standing to face him head on. "Family all okay, parents reasonably happy, I had some alright friends, all that nice shit. Then we fast forward to four months ago, when there was about a week of spending all day, *every day*, at the hospital."

His expression had softened now and he took another step towards me.

"Anna..."

But I ignored him, taking a step back from him, unable to stop the words from falling out of me.

"Okay, so we had a week, near enough. Sleeping in a chair next to my brother's hospital bed, holding his hand. Calling out his name, hoping that he might respond. Hospital dinners from the canteen. My parents, crying, *clutching* at each other." I was surprised at how steady my voice was coming out, how little it wavered or shook.

"Doctors giving us hourly updates, trying to give us hope when there was none." I was breathing heavily now, my chest feeling tight. "There was none."

His eyes were brimming with guilt. "Your brother." he whispered.

I nodded blankly. "Motorbike accident. He'd only had it a week." I sighed, feeling like something was rattling in my chest. "My best friend."

He took a couple more steps towards me, his arms limp by his sides. I pressed my lips together in a tight line, willing myself to keep my shit together.

"Yeah so then there was the funeral, obviously. Lots of people hugging me. Friends checking in. University sending out emails every day saying how sorry they were, how they *understood*." I laughed humourlessly, shaking my head.

"After that..." I shrugged. "Parents tried but, I mean..." I took a deep breath. "It was clear pretty early on that they weren't going to be able to get each other through it. That they weren't going to be able to get *me* through it."

He was only a step away from me now, looking down at me through the gentlest of eyes. The silver of them seemed to swim in my vision, blurring with the tears that were beginning to fill my eyes.

"Then the last couple of months?" I shook my head. "People stop texting, stop calling. University gets *less* empathetic. Not that I even really give a shit, anymore."

He reached out for me with a steady, translucent hand, wrapping his fingers around my wrist and rubbing soft circles at the base of my palm.

"My life is bed. Eating, when I can make myself. Watching hours – shit, *days* of TV that I don't give a shit about. Forgetting to shower."

The tears were getting dangerously close to spilling over now and the sensation of his reassuring fingers on my hand was making my breath catch painfully in my chest.

"Praying, or pleading with a God that I don't even fucking *believe* in, that I've *never* believed in..." I was blubbering now, chest rising and falling unpredictably. "Just in some mad hope that it might bring him back to me."

Before I knew what was happening, he was pulling me by the wrist into his arms. He wrapped them around my shoulders and I rested my head on his chest. I could feel his hand in my hair like silk, brushing the strands. I could feel the weight of his arms around me, when I knew I shouldn't be able to. I could feel the way he tightened his hold on me when I shuddered out a sob that I couldn't contain any longer. I could feel my tears soaking into his body that wasn't even really there.

"Anna, I'm so sorry." he murmured into my hair, his voice wracked with anguish.

I closed my eyes and pushed back from him a few inches, matching my eyes to his. They melted into me, the most real and unreal things I had ever seen. He held my hands between our bodies and I looked up to him.

"Things were fucked before you got here." I said, trying not to let my tears override the sincerity of my words. "You think you made things worse, but..." I shook my head. "They were already at worse. They were the minute that I lost Charlie. There was no further for me to go."

He let go of one of my hands and wiped away one of the tears away from my cheek. He kept his thumb there for a moment, holding my face in his hand of silk. I think it's the most intimate thing that I've ever experienced. Deep in my chest, something felt like it was about to fracture.

"I'm not scared." I said firmly, putting force behind these words, knowing that he needed to hear them. "It doesn't scare me that you're here, or that I can see through you. It doesn't scare me that I'm the only thing that you can touch. It doesn't scare me that I'm the only one that can see you, or that you're…"

"A ghost." he whispered softly.

It's the first time that either of us have admitted it aloud.

I nodded slowly. "A ghost." I breathed out quietly. "I don't care that it's confusing, or mind-bending, or doesn't make any sense. You're *here* and I… I don't have to be…" I ducked my head down, feeling the tears beginning to well in my eyes again, unable to stop them from falling on the rug beneath us. "I just, I don't want to be…"

He held my chin gently with his thumb and forefinger, tipping my face up to look into his eyes again. Everything in his face was mournful, understanding. The silver of his eyelashes caught the light and glowed warmly.

"It's okay, I know, I know." he whispered, pulling me into him again. He rested his chin on the top of my head and I thought I felt him place a soft kiss there, gentle and sweet. I wrapped my arms around his torso, revelling in how the silk of his body felt.

"I'm here, okay?" he murmured, rocking me back and forth slowly until the tears began to subside. "I'm here."

You don't have to be alone anymore.

HIM

Hours later, in the darkness, Anna was lying next to me on top of her bed. Her breathing had slowed to a calm rhythm now and her eyelids were dropping closed, heavy with sleep.

"Anna?" I whispered out to her across the bed.

"Mmm?" she answered sleepily.

"What should we do?" I asked quietly. "About me?"

She shifted around a little, bringing her face closer to mine.

"Well, we have all these questions, right?" she asked softly.

I nodded silently. She shrugged lightly, casting her eyes over my face.

"Maybe we should stop asking questions and start looking for some answers." she said in a low voice.

I lay awake that night, next to her sleeping body on the bed, staring up at the ceiling. Thinking of the questions I needed answering and whether if the answers came, I would even want to hear them.

CHAPTER 5

ANNA

A SMALL DEGREE of normality was granted to us after we realised that we could move about the world as we pleased, without anyone seeing him – without the questions that we had anticipated, or the shock or fear that we were sure the sight of him would cause.

He found now, that he could even leave my bedroom and move about the house at will. It was as if the universe now trusted him not to run away... or maybe even just get lost. It was like we had been forced together at the start.

I let him come with me everywhere. After our trip to the woods, he was eager to experience as much as possible. Even the small and mundane seemed to fill him with joy. That being said, we established that it was definitely more comfortable for us to be alone, where we could be free to talk to each other, away from the suspicious looks that were cast in my direction when people assumed that I was talking to *myself*. It didn't help, of course, that when I would try not to interact with him in public, he would make little funny comments, desperate to make me laugh.

Once, when a particularly moody and stern-looking cashier was scanning some shopping, he'd stood beside me, grinning straight at her. She, of course, had absolutely no inkling that he was even there. When she slammed down a packet of rice like it had personally offended her, he couldn't help himself from commenting on it.

"My God," he'd said, laughing lightly, "someone needs to tell this lady that it's nearly the weekend."

I'd refused to look at him – just pressed my lips into a straight line to stop myself from laughing and shook my head lightly. He'd looked to me and grinned, sensing a challenge.

"No, you're right," he said, turning his head back to her, "it's not funny. She's got a nice way about her, actually."

She chucked down a pint of milk, nearly causing the bottle-top to come off. I threw him a sideways glance as if to say, *please don't*. But the corners of his mouth were turned up in a teasing smile.

"What? I'm just saying," he said, feigning innocence, "I'm seriously thinking about going home with Mrs Chuckles, here tonight, instead of you."

I couldn't help myself any longer. I had to turn my head away to laugh, causing the cashier to jump slightly, then fix me with a withering scowl before carrying on scanning my items.

"You're unbelievable." I whispered to him as we left the shop, but I was smiling even as I said it.

HIM

"Sometimes it feels like you're a figment of my imagination." Anna said to me that afternoon, while she was curled up on the sofa in the lounge, feet tucked underneath her. "Like maybe I made you up."
I frowned over at her. "It feels like that?"
She nodded. "Especially when we're outside and

nobody else can see you. It feels like you're just here for me."

Would that be so bad? I considered saying, but thought better of it. I took a deep breath.

"Like an imaginary friend?" I asked.

She shrugged. "Do you think that's possible?"

I thought for a moment, then shook my head.

"I don't think so. Even if only you can see me, I'm still *real*. I mean, I feel real, at least. Imaginary friends can't ever be this tangible, I don't think."

She nodded at this, her eyes glazing over for a moment, lost in thought.

"I didn't think ghosts could ever be this tangible, either." She reached her hand across the expanse of the sofa, searching for mine. Without even thinking, I wrapped her pale skin up in my bigger, translucent hands.

"Makes you think, doesn't it? About what else could be real, things that we might have just written off as impossible–"

"I know." she murmured absentmindedly, watching our hands with tired eyes. "God, I really hope mermaids are real."

I couldn't help but laugh at this, gazing down at her face, where a small smile was setting in.

"I'm serious." she said, looking up at me, green eyes light and playful, "And vampires. As long as they're hot, obviously. And fairies and witches, and–"

She stopped suddenly, sitting up straight, her eyebrows furrowed together in deep concentration.

"What?" I asked, resting back on the sofa so that I could see her better.

Her eyes were lit with glee when she finally turned to me, a wide grin lighting up the rest of her face.

"I've got an idea."

ANNA

"I'm a genius." I said later that evening, stood next to him in front of a well-lit shopfront, on one of the backstreets of the town centre.

We both stood there for a moment, heads tilted upwards to the glowing sign above us, which read in large neon letters – *A GUIDING LIGHT*. Another neon sign in the shape of an open palm was hanging in the left window, casting a red light to warm his ghostly form.

"This is the worst idea ever." he said slowly, staring up at the sign with apprehensive eyes.

I laughed at him, shaking my head at his obvious disdain.

"Come on, you have to at least be a little bit curious." I grinned at him.

He turned to me, incredulous. "I can't believe you're even considering this! Anna, you *have* to know that all of this is a scam."

"Of course, yeah. The same way that I know that *ghosts* aren't real?" I challenged.

He opened his mouth to speak, then seemed to think better of it.

I smiled, knowing that I was winning.

"Come on, let's just go in! The worst that's going to happen is that she can't see you, just like *everybody else*. And I'm out twenty quid." I shrugged and he looked down at me, unconvinced. "Not a big deal."

He threw his head back in annoyance and I smiled, grabbing his wrist and pulling him into the shop before he could protest again.

Windchimes sounded out as we walked through the door and into a small room, lit only by two small lamps and a few candles dotted about the room. I was immediately hit with the smell of incense, which I had sort of expected, but was still a nice sensation. I had expected the room to be crowded – stacked full of the typical witchy stuff that tourists get so attached to – bowls of crystals, old tea-soaked spell books and so on. But I was pleasantly surprised as I cast my eyes around the room, which was decorated simply and elegantly. A huge wooden bookshelf stood against the far wall, covered from top to bottom in books of all shapes and sizes. A dark orange sofa sat in the corner of the room, with a small coffee table and a couple of cosy looking armchairs.

I glanced over at him, where his translucency was causing his body to take on almost all of the candlelight in the room, making him look warm and almost as real as I'd ever seen him. I gave him a look to say – *see, doesn't look so bad, does it?*

He shook his head at me and moved over to inspect the books on the shelf, muttering quietly. "Fine, she gets brownie points for not having any crystal balls hanging around, at least."

Before I could think about replying, a beaded curtain to the right of the bookshelf opened and he froze up completely, rigid and silent.

A small lady tottered through the gap in the beads and straight past him, oblivious to his ghostly form.

She focused her eyes on me and smiled warmly. She may have been one of the shortest women I'd ever seen in my life, standing nearly a foot shorter than even me. Soft wrinkles adorned her kind face, showing signs of many years of laughter. Her grey hair was tied up with a red ribbon at the back of her head and she wore a dark red jumper that looked extremely sweet on her tiny frame.

"Hello, my dear." she said in a quiet voice, sweet and gentle. I saw him look over to me then and my eyes flickered to him.

He sighed. "Alright, she's cute."

Ignoring him, I smiled down at the charming lady and said, "Hi, it's nice to meet you. I'm Anna."

When her hand shook mine, I was overwhelmed by a calm feeling, as though her soft skin against mine was soothing something deep inside me.

"I'm Laurie." she said, smiling at me again. "Why don't you sit down and I'll make us some tea?"

So I moved to the orange sofa whilst she disappeared behind the beaded curtain and he came to sit next to me, shifting a little in his seat.

"I like her." I whispered, turning my head to him for a moment.

He smiled, but I knew it was only to humour me. "She can't see me."

I shrugged and whispered back, "I still like her."

He placed his arm along the back of the sofa so that his hand was only an inch or so from my hair. I thought I saw his fingers twitch a little.

Laurie came back then, holding an ornate tray with two small teacups on it and I stood to help her serve the cups. Then she settled down opposite the two of us in one of her patchwork armchairs, warm brown eyes fixed me as I stirred my tea.

"Um, without sounding offensive, you're not exactly what I expected." I said slowly, trying to gauge her reaction.

But she merely laughed – a soft melodic sound and raised her eyebrows amusedly. "Well, you aren't what I expected either, darling."

I cocked my head to the side, frowning in silent question. Next to me, I could feel his silver eyes darting back and forth between the two of us, observing.

"You're very young." she offered simply and something small inside my chest ached.

I smiled. "Doesn't feel that way, sometimes."

His eyes were fixed on me now, I could feel his gaze boring into me. Before I could stop myself, I skirted along the sofa a little, so I was sat closer to him. We didn't touch, but I liked how it felt to have him within reach.

Laurie smiled gently, seemingly oblivious to all of this.

"And are you a sceptic?" She took a sip of the tea, eyes never moving from me.

I started a little, unsure of what to say. "N-no. I mean yes, I was." I shook my head, trying to get my thoughts straight. "I don't know, anymore."

She nodded as if she understood, as if what I had said wasn't at all cryptic.

"And why are you here?" she asked, leaning back, stirring her tea hypnotically.

I sighed, considering her question. He leaned

forward next to me, resting his arms on his knees and looked back at me, encouraging me with his eyes.

"I guess I'm just hoping that you know more than I do. That you *understand* more than I do."

She nodded again, knowingly, like this had been what she'd expected from me all along. Her eyes were all sincerity as they swept over me.

"I understand that you have lost someone." It was barely above a whisper, but still enough to make my breath catch in my chest.

The candlelight flickered again. I wanted to look to him, but I couldn't. I didn't want to cry.

"Yes." It was all I could say and still it made my voice shake.

He sighed audibly next to me and reached out his transparent hand to hold mine, safe in his silk touch.

Laurie seemed to draw back in her chair for a moment, her eyes flitting to where my hand rested on the sofa, inside of his. Then she raised her eyes to stare at the space next to me, where *he* sat. Her eyes were wider and full of wonder, but there wasn't a trace of fear. And they were fixed on him.

She was looking *straight at him*. He gripped my hand a little tighter, frozen still in his surprise. My heart felt as though it had stopped beating entirely.

She just smiled. "But you are not alone."

HIM

I couldn't move. I couldn't speak. *I had to speak.*
"Uh, Anna…" I stuttered, holding the older lady's gaze, unblinking, "Can… can she…"

Laurie laughed, all sunshine, seemingly unfazed. "I

can see you, my darling. And hear you, clear as you can hear me, I'm sure."

Anna whipped her head around to gawk at me, then back to Laurie, completely gobsmacked.

"Laurie, you're the first – I mean, I thought I was the only one who could see him."

"I'm quite sure you were, dear." Laurie muttered softly, casting her eyes all over my form, her expression one of pure curiosity. "Perhaps not, anymore though."

Anna breathed something that half sounded like laughing, half like a sigh of relief. I finally found my voice, encouraged by the comforting feeling of her hand in mine.

"How can you see me?" I asked, leaning forward.

Laurie frowned for a moment, the creases in her skin deepening. She ran her eyes over me again and I tried not to feel uncomfortable under her gaze. I ran my thumb over Anna's knuckles distractedly and Laurie looked down to our hands again, eyes latching onto the sight.

"The touch…" she whispered quietly, more to herself than in answer. I frowned to Anna, who was looking at Laurie with pure astonishment.

But Laurie had abandoned that train of thought, shaking her head lightly and started to smile at us both again.

"I'm sure that is not the question you are here to ask, young man." She laughed lightly, leaning back in her chair.

She was right. Suddenly, my mind had filled to the brim with questions that I wanted to ask, answers that I was desperately seeking. So many questions that my brain was tripping over them all and I couldn't put any of them together in the right way.

"Have you ever seen this happen before?" I managed to get out after a while.

"Once or twice, yes. It's rare, but…" Laurie paused for a moment, giving me a gentle smile, "people sometimes get stuck in between, you see."

Anna took a sharp breath in. "In between what?" she asked, her voice full of apprehension.

Everything in the room was still for a moment, as though the whole world was holding its breath.

Laurie's brown eyes filled with sympathy. We both knew what she was going to say. But in a way, we both needed to hear the words.

"In between life and what comes after, my love." She did not direct her answer towards Anna, but towards me.

Laurie bent her head down in a slow nod to me, as if to say *I'm sorry*. Offering her condolences. I tried to smile and managed the barest whisper of one.

I couldn't look at Anna, who had turned towards me, gripping my hand tightly in hers.

"I, uh…" I shook my head, trying to get my thoughts together, "I can't remember who I was. Before. I can't remember anything."

Laurie seemed surprised at this and leaned back in her chair to consider it. Anna, ever-impatient, noticed this immediately and could not help but interrupt her thoughts.

"Is that not normal?" she asked quickly, all wild inquisitiveness.

Laurie drew in a sharp breath and leaned forward

again, eyes glancing between the two of us.

"Dearest, we are talking about ghosts and spirits, life and afterlife." She shook her head lightly, eyes full of laughter. "There is no *normal*. That being said…" Her soft eyes returned to mine again, looking through me, "It isn't something I have ever encountered before."

"And the fact that only I can see him?" Anna inquired further.

"Of course, it's quite common that those who are stuck are only able to be seen by one person. Those who can see them were usually their nearest and dearest, in life."

"But we'd never met, even when he was alive." Anna interjected.

Laurie frowned. "You're quite sure?"

Anna nodded firmly.

Laurie paused for a moment. "There are things that can keep a person stuck in between." she began slowly, considering her words carefully. "Specific to the individual, of course. A loose thread." Laurie caught my eyes then, holding my gaze steadily. "A purpose."

A heart that I didn't have was thrumming inside my chest. I couldn't breathe for the pressure pushing at me from all angles. Laurie did not look away until Anna spoke again.

"But you don't know what it could be?" Her voice was tinged with slight disappointment.

Laurie's eyes flicked back to mine and Anna's hands, clasped together tightly on the sofa, then up to my eyes.

I shook my head a minute amount, pleading with her through my eyes.

Please, don't. Not yet.

Laurie turned her eyes back to Anna, who was leaning forward, eager for answers.

"Well, how could I possibly, when I don't know who the young man was?"

Her light-hearted smile was fake; behind it I could see the sorrow fighting to surface. But Anna was oblivious, which was all that mattered.

"But if we could figure it out," Anna began again, determined to follow this thread to its eventual end, "figure out who he was, I mean…"

Laurie shrugged gently. "In theory, some closure…" Her eyes darted towards me for a moment and I swallowed hard, feeling her lie punch into my chest, making my eyes water, "it could set him free and send him onwards."

Anna leaned back into the sofa, lost to her thoughts. "Closure…" she muttered softly to herself.

"Of course, one can never be sure of these things." Laurie added softly, holding my grey eyes with her brown ones.

"Of course," I said in response, hoping to add a little lightness to the conversation. "I mean, technically I shouldn't even be here. Could just be some sort of cosmic glitch, right?"

Laurie smiled, all warmth. "Even the cosmos is capable of mistakes."

But Anna was shaking her head, eyes drawn to me again, hand still firmly held in mine.

"I don't think so." she replied quietly, "I think there's a reason. We just have to find it."

I smiled at her then, chest aching beyond belief.

Not yet. Let there be a few more days of bliss.

Laurie seemed sad to see us go, all melancholic smiles and clasping Anna's hands with compassion, thanking her for coming. She wished us all the best and encouraged us to come back to her, if ever we felt the need.

"Thank you," Anna had replied, eyes full of sincerity and gratitude.

When she turned away from the small lady, I moved in front of her, holding her gaze once again.

"*Thank you.*" I said, putting emphasis behind my words, wanting her to know that I appreciated her discretion. Laurie gave me a knowing smile and bowed her head towards me again, slight and subtle.

I gave her my most genuine smile and Anna and I turned for the door.

Just as the tinkle of the windchimes rang out through the shop, Laurie called out to us.

"Anna!" The small lady wrapped her arms around her middle and gave a sigh, "I'm so sorry, my darling. About your brother."

I felt the breath get taken away from Anna's lungs as she stood still, next to me. The cold breeze from the street blew her hair around her face. She frowned at Laurie at first, confused as to how she knew, but then smiled sadly, deciding to let it go.

"Thank you, Laurie. Goodnight." she said softly, and we ducked out of the door with a small wave in her direction.

We stood still for a moment, rooted to the ground outside of the shop. Anna gazed up at me, a look of tired satisfaction on her face.

"So?" she asked, a small smile playing at her lips, "What do you think?"

I laughed wryly, shaking my head in pure disbelief. I smiled back at Anna, wrapping my arm around her shoulder, steering her back in the direction of home.

"Well for starters, she should definitely charge more."

Anna was quiet on the way home, but her thoughts seemed to fill the car from window to window.

"What are you thinking?" I asked tentatively, when I could no longer bear the silence.

She sighed softly, drumming her fingers on the steering wheel distractedly.

"All that stuff she said, about being stuck in between… what comes after…" She trailed off, quiet and contemplative.

With a jolt, I suddenly realised where her thoughts were.

She shook her head, eyes fixed on the road ahead. "I hope that's not Charlie. I hope he's not–"

"He's not." I said, before I even knew what I was saying.

Anna looked over to me, eyes wide with surprise. "How do you know?"

I took a deep breath. "If he was, I'm sure it would be him here right now, not me."

She considered this for a moment, then nodded. We were silent for a moment, but it was comfortable.

"I miss him so much." she whispered, barely able to get it out.

Something was pulling at my stomach when I looked at her, green eyes full of tears that were ready to spill over, her pale hands gripping the steering wheel with an intensity I hadn't seen before.

"Will you tell me about him?" I asked, softly.

She drew in a ragged breath, held it for a moment, then let it out slowly. "No."

Her eyes stayed looking forward. I observed her for a moment, then nodded, reaching over to lay a comforting hand on her arm. She didn't mean 'no'. What she really meant was, 'not yet'.

The wind blew through the cracked window of the car, uncaring about our troubles, whipping her hair around her face again. As one of the tears escaped, leaving a track down her cheek, she turned her head to me for a moment, sending me a small apologetic smile.

"It's okay." I said in reply, reaching out to wipe the stray tear away from her face.

I could wait.

Anna took a while to fall asleep that night. Excited by the prospect of new information, of answers, she was high on the events of the evening. Every now and then she would sit bolt upright in her bed, eyes wildly searching for the shape of me in her room, wanting to discuss a new avenue of our next steps. She had ideas, theories on how to get the information about my old life that she now thought we needed.

When she eventually slept, her voice rang around the hollow hallways of my mind.

All of this could be explained, if we could just figure out who you were before. We could find out what's keeping you here.

Laurie said you just need some closure.
You deserve to know who you are.

Of course, in some ways she was entirely right.

I was *desperate* to know who I was. My name, my age, my friends, family, hobbies. The music I liked. The books I read. The people I cared about. All these things were being kept an arm's length away from me, no matter how much I reached out for them, they evaded my touch.

Most of the time I felt like I was swimming in a vast lake, entirely out of my depth. But every time I thought I could see a glimpse of the lake's edge and started moving towards it, it was gone again and all I could see for miles was water. I wanted to get out of the water, to walk along its edge and *know* where I was, know *who* I was. I wanted to piece myself together, to make myself whole again.

But in other ways, she was entirely wrong.

What Anna didn't know – what I was burdened to one day tell her – was that finding these things, piecing me together, was not going to bring me the closure that she thought it would. Knowing my past would not let me move on to whatever else was waiting for me. Laurie was right, there *was* something keeping me stuck in between life and 'the after'. But in my chest, I knew that it wasn't anything to do with my old life, whatever it had been. The loose thread wasn't *me*.

It was Anna.

Hers was the voice that I had reached out to in the dark, before she even knew I was there. *She* was the force that was keeping me there, my body withering away without her presence, then her touch reviving me – making me the most alive I can remember feeling. I was only able to exist where she was – only able to leave the room when her touch unlocked it. Only seen by her, unless her touch allowed me to be seen by another. Her body was the only thing that felt *real* to me and allowed me to feel real in return.

However strange it was, I was certain that the loose thread that Laurie had spoken of had Anna tied at one end and me grasping desperately at the other end. I was here for her, because however much she tried to push it away, or cover it with harsh words, or bury it under excuses, she needed someone. She *needed* not to be alone.

Anna had called out in the night, through tears heavy with desperation and I had answered. I didn't know how, or why. All I knew was that my purpose was *this*. I hadn't realised it at the time, but I had chosen my fate that night. And I would choose it again, if I had to.

Anna's body stirred in sleep and I took an uneven breath.

The fact was that, though she had no idea, the power was in her hands. If she wanted me to go, I assumed that all she had to do was let go of her end of the thread.

Deep down, I knew that I was being selfish by keeping the truth from her. For weeks I'd told myself that the time wasn't right for her to know – I hadn't helped her enough with her grief yet, she'd barely even begun to open up to me the way that she needed to. She was still in pain, still in denial. I was going to be there for her, holding her hand, until she didn't need me anymore. Besides, I didn't want to go 'on' without first knowing everything, knowing *myself*.

But underneath it all, I was scared. Scared that if she knew the truth, she'd *want* to send me away. That being alone would be the preferable option to all the complications, the stress, the confusion that I brought to her life. I was keeping it from her not just for *her* sake, but for mine as well.

It filled my body with cold, hard guilt to even think it, but I wasn't ready to let go of her yet. Even worse, I was terrified that she might want to let go of me and I wasn't ready for that either.

The secret lay heavy in the pit of my stomach as I watched her sleep. It was like a venomous snake curled up inside me, lying in wait, ready to strike and ruin everything that meant anything to me.

Every time I closed my eyes, I saw Anna ravelling and unravelling a loose thread around her finger, looking up at me with her big green eyes.

Ravelling and unravelling.

Ravelling and unravelling.

CHAPTER 6

ANNA

"So, what do we actually know *for sure*, about you?"

His ethereal face stared at me, blankly. "Nothing."

It was two days since we'd visited Laurie and we were sitting next to each other in the kitchen doorway, staring into the garden. The rain was pouring down uncontrollably, and every now and then a drop would fall onto my arm, making my hairs stand on end.

Since meeting Laurie, I couldn't stop my brain from ticking and theorising about ways to discover his real identity. Of course, there were obvious holes in my plans – the fact that he remembered absolutely nothing and I in turn had no idea who he might have been either. But the situation was far from hopeless, I had decided. There were a few things that we knew and those were the places to start.

"Not true." I replied, shaking my head. "Think about it."

He blinked a couple of times, which I was beginning to recognise as a nervous reflex, rather than him actually needing to blink. Then he frowned, considering my words.

He'd been enthusiastic about the idea of searching for his identity, contributing to my ideas whenever he could suggest something. Despite this, I couldn't help feeling like he was holding something back from me, or even from himself. There was something guarded in his eyes each time we spoke about it and he would never hold my gaze for as long as I wanted him to.

He didn't want to get his hopes up. He didn't want to put too much pressure on finding himself, just in case we couldn't. His entire existence, his purpose, was hinged on this – a blind investigation, where we had nothing to go on.

Well, *almost* nothing.

"We know what you look like." I pointed out, nodding towards his form, sitting cross legged on the kitchen floor.

He peered down at himself, giving a full inspection. "Not much to go on, really. Against all this white tiling, I basically look like a glass of water."

I laughed, shaking my head at him.

He was wrong. Despite having less colour to him against the harsh white of the kitchen, he was still perfectly visible and looked about as ghostly as he ever had. Silver, like a sculpture carved out of some crystal. The rain fell through his hands as he held them in the doorway and I couldn't help but smile. Even like this, he was beautiful.

"Okay, but we could still recognise you, if we saw a picture." I softened my voice slightly, glancing at him. "And… we know when you died."

He sat up straight at these words and turned to look at me fully. A soft crease appeared between his brows.

"Do we?" His voice was low and confused.

Suddenly feeling self-conscious, my eyes fell to my lap and when I spoke, my voice was full of caution.

"Well, we know the date that you first appeared here. It wouldn't be too far of a stretch to assume that you died around then, right?"

He considered for a moment. A breeze whipped a few droplets of rain onto my face, and before I could wipe them away, he had already raised his hand to do the same thing. Once they were gone, his fingers lingered for a moment too long on my cheek and he cast his silver eyes over my face gently. When I caught his eyes, he cleared his throat a little and dropped his hand back to his side.

"I guess not. I mean, I don't know for sure, but it seems to make sense." he murmured, staring out to the rain again.

I nodded my head firmly, trying to push the memory of his silk skin against mine out of my head.

"So, um..." I started, then tried again, "I think we should search for deaths around that time, that date. If there are articles, there might be pictures–"

"It might have been reported." he interrupted, nodding his head slowly.

I tried to catch his eye, but they stayed fixed on the silver birch tree in the garden, swaying wildly in the wind and rain. When he didn't look at me, I tentatively moved my hand to his back, stroking a line up and down it. This made him sigh softly and he eventually tore his eyes away from the tree to look at me again.

"You're nervous?" I asked, speaking as gently as I could.

He smiled, but it didn't reach his eyes. "To find out how I died through a news article?" He shook his head in disbelief. "Why would I be?"

My stomach nearly turned over at his words and I suddenly couldn't believe how insensitive this all was.

I sighed, watching him carefully. He was looking out into the rain again, this time up at the clouds, moving rapidly over us in the wind.

"We don't have to do this." I started, but he was shaking his head.

"We do." he said simply, eyes never moving from the clouds overhead.

We spent all day wrapped up in the covers, searching for any evidence of his death on the internet. The wind beat at the windows as we looked, rain covering the panes in sheets.

"So, assuming that I did die the night uh, before, I appeared here," he began, scratching his head awkwardly, "then my date of death would be..."

"October 25th?" I suggested, working back the weeks in my head.

And so we scoured the internet for information. It was certainly no small task – thousands, or tens of thousands of people die *every day*, even just in Britain. We sifted through the reports of tragic accidents, gruesome crimes and heart-breaking illness one by one, eliminating them based on what we knew of him.

"Too old." I would say,

Or, "Too young."

Frustratingly, even after we'd found a few instances where the dead had seemed to be around the same age as him, after a few more minutes research into them, we would always find pictures on different articles, or on social media.

And he would say, "He doesn't look much like me, does he?"

Or, "Definitely too tall."

Or, "I *wish* I'd looked like that guy."

As the daylight began to fade from the room and darkness settled in, our hope for finding what we were looking for seemed to fade along with it.

After a couple of hours of filtering through the last few reports of the dead, he let out a huge sigh and laid back on the bed, shutting his eyes tightly for a moment.

"None of them are me." he said flatly, his eyes still closed. "We sorted through all the ones we could find from the right date and either they aren't my age, or they look nothing like me."

I sighed along with him, unable to deny the truth behind his words. Sweeping my hair over my shoulder, I let myself fall back to lie on the bed next to him, our shoulders pressed against each other firmly. I could feel the shape of his arm, solid and real, next to mine on the bed and had to stop myself from reaching out to touch it.

"No, none of them are you." I sighed, turning on my side so that I could see him better. "Are you disappointed?"

He turned on his side then too, body mirroring mine on the bed. Only inches away from me, he opened his eyes and searched my face, considering my question.

"I don't even know…" he whispered in a faraway voice.

I wanted to take this from him, this feeling. Even though he hadn't let himself hope, I could see that the feeling of utter loss that filled him now was in some ways worse than disappointment. He was all the way back at the beginning, with no end in sight.

"Can I tell you something?" I said quietly, catching his eyes with mine.

"Mmm?"

I shook my head a little, holding his gaze. "I'm not disappointed, that we didn't find you like that." I murmured, bringing my hand up to his face, tracing the lines of his features with my fingertip. "I wouldn't have wanted to read about your death, all cold and fact-like. Not like that, you…"

He frowned at me a little, unable to predict what I was going to say. My heartbeat was rising steadily with him being this close to me and I had to swallow my nerves in order to continue.

"You deserve more." I said simply.

At this he smiled, his eyes full of emotion. The clouds broke apart in anguish when he spoke.

"What if this was our only shot at knowing, though?"

"Does it feel like it was?" I asked, trying to get an idea of how he was really feeling.

Something stirred in him for a moment as he thought to himself.

"I don't think so. It never felt right." he said after a moment, searching my eyes for a reaction. I merely nodded, holding his gaze steadily. "We were trying to apply logic to it, to figuring this all out."

Ghostly fingers traced a line up and down my arm and he watched them as he thought. I tried to focus on his words, rather than on the sensation of his velvety fingers on my skin, causing all my nerves to become alert.

"But…?" I prompted him. His eyes flashed to mine

and he licked his lips distractedly, then looked back to his fingertips on my arm.

"But maybe," he shrugged, "maybe this isn't the sort of thing you can apply logic to. Maybe it's more complicated than that."

"Or more simple." I countered. The silver in his eyes seemed to darken to grey and he nodded in response.

"Maybe." he said.

Nothing in that moment made any sense. Nothing but the feeling of his skin, touching mine.

HIM

Everything inside me felt shallow that evening, nearly empty. Anna went for a bath and I sat without her on the bed, staring at the television in the corner of the room, barely registering what the actors were even saying. Outside, the rain hadn't let up for even a second, still casting fleeting shadows on the walls of Anna's room as it fell.

We weren't going to find me.

I floated about Anna's room, rolling the idea over and over in my mind. Letting it stretch out my brain and consider all the implications. *I might never know who I am.*

I might never see my parents, who are out there somewhere, looking like me. I'd never see *my* bedroom – what posters hung on the walls, what books crowded the shelves. Anna, beautiful, wild Anna, might never call me by my name.

I'm only a fraction of a man. I'll never be whole.

When Anna comes back, all soft and warm and filling the room with light again, the emptiness seems to subside a little and I am at least able to smile. She's wearing her red pattered pyjama shorts and a tiny black t-shirt on top and her cheeks are a little flushed with warmth when she smiles back at me. Her dark hair falls in damp curls around her shoulders, grazing the small of her back when she walks.

She is heaven, and when she speaks it takes me a while to even register her words, because all I can think is that she is standing *too far* away from me. I need her to be closer.

"What?" I say, making her smile in a confused way.

"I just said, I'm surprisingly tired."

I nodded automatically. "Me too."

She frowned, running her fingers through her hair to work through the tangles. "You don't sleep."

I laughed and shrugged, moving off the bed to take my place on her window-ledge like I did every night. "Doesn't mean I'm not tired."

She smiled sadly and nodded, sitting atop her bed and switching off one of the lamps so that darkness enveloped one side of the room. I drew my knees up to my chest and peered through the window, watching a small grey cat on the other side of the road take shelter from the rain under a car. I focused on the sound of Anna's breathing, like I did every night. Most nights, after a few minutes the breaths would deepen and slow and from then it would only be a little while longer before she would be asleep.

But tonight, her breathing didn't deepen. In fact, the more I listened, the more it sounded like her breath was catching in her chest, like the more she tried to sleep, the more worked up she was getting.

My legs carried me to her, before my head could say no. I stood for a moment over her, realising that her eyes were actually open. She turned to lie on her back, facing me. Her green eyes latched onto mine and she silently pulled the sheet back for me to climb into bed with her.

I did so without hesitation, wrapping my arm around her shoulders so that she could tuck her body into mine. With her pressed against me, I felt the warmth of life spread through me, over and over. I breathed a sigh of relief as I felt myself settle with her, finally beginning to feel real, solid, *there*.

I ran my hand through her hair, catching a few of the long dark strands between my fingers and marvelling at them. She hummed softy at the sensation and the sound shot a jolt so significant through me that I forgot how to breathe.

Anna's head rested on my chest and her eyes closed for a moment. Then her arm reached out for mine and she ran her finger up and down the inside of my forearm, leaving trails of warmth where her fingers passed.

"Anna, Anna…" I whispered into her hair, not really sure what I was saying.

Everything was overwhelming – I could *feel* everything. It was weighty and warm and I could feel her beating heart against my ribs, feel her body keeping me grounded, finally tying me down to the earth with her.

"I know." she whispered back, turning her head to look up at me. Her eyes were full of something that I couldn't recognise.

I held her face in my hand, only centimetres away from mine. I wasn't empty anymore – I was real and *present* and full of her, overcome with her. I held her gaze for a moment.

"Are you scared of me?" I asked her quietly, my eyes dropping to her lips for a moment before coming back to her eyes, wide and green and looking at me with everything she had.

"Yes." she said and there was nothing but honesty in her words.

I could feel the speeding beat of her pulse when my fingers grazed her neck.

"Are you scared of *me?*" she whispered at me, searching my face.

It was almost physically painful, having her so close and battling the need to have her even closer. With each passing second I was fighting another impulse to pull her in tighter, weave my fingers in her hair and capture her lips in mine, or interlace my fingers through hers and hold them tightly, so she'd never let go.

I smiled at her, because I couldn't not smile at her.

"Terrified." I whispered honestly, something splintering in my chest as I said it.

We didn't speak for a moment. We just laid there together, taking in one another in quiet awe. Anna's eyes flickered over my face, as if she were trying to memorise every line of me. Long, dark eyelashes brushed against her cheeks when her eyes fell to my lips and back up again.

"How are you real?" I asked, before I had the sense to stop myself.

She drew her head back a little, surprised by my words.

"How are *you?*" she breathed, but there was no laughter in her words.

The rain continued to beat against the windows, but I could barely even hear it anymore. Everything, all the sounds in the room, they were all her. Her heart beating, her breath drawing me in and out, her voice sweeping over my skin as though it were real. As though *I* were real. She laid her head on my chest and I let her, revelling in how the weight of her felt.

"Can you really feel me?" I whispered to her, barely audible.

I felt her nod against my chest. She lifted her head up to look at me again, frowning a little.

"Always." I said, before she could even ask. "I can always feel you. Even when we aren't touching. All you have to do is walk into the room."

My fingers were in her hair, the strands ravelling around me like threads of silk. Her green eyes were dark and light all at once.

When I kissed her it was sudden, but I'd also been waiting my entire life.

Her perfect porcelain face was cradled in my hands and the feeling of her lips against mine was like *nothing* I'd ever felt before. When she pressed back against me, bringing her hands to my hair and running her fingers through it, I could think of nothing but her. The taste of her was intoxicating and when she hummed contently against my lips heat shot to the back of my neck and I couldn't help but weave my free hand into hers, gripping it tightly and clinging to her.

I am whole. I was wrong. I am whole.

Her breath hitched a little and I pulled back instinctively, still holding her face only centimetres away from mine.

I waited for a moment, just holding her there. Everything about this moment, the way the air hung around us, the way the silence wrapped its fingers around our shoulders, was delicate. We were delicate.

"Was that a mistake?" I asked after a little while, tracing my thumb over her cheek.

"No." she murmured quietly, her eyes dropping to my lips again. The lie swept me in and shrouded me in a warmth that I knew I didn't deserve.

Anna moved even closer to me, pressing her forehead against mine and taking a deep breath. Beside us, her hand held mine even tighter.

ANNA

When morning came and the sunlight streamed through the gap in my curtains, I held his hand up to it, marvelling at the way that the light made him an angel in front of my eyes.

We spent the morning in bed, not needing to go anywhere. For now, there was nothing more important than this – exploring the sense of touch in a capacity that neither of us had ever felt before. My hands, wrapped up in his, hazy like half-formed silk, but real. My skin against his. The vibration of his chest when he spoke my name. My lips against his, confusing and dizzying and–

"Consuming." he laughed softly, his fingertips tracing a line up the curve of my hipbone. "This could consume me. This feeling."

I smiled at his words, unable to keep my heart from stopping for a moment in my chest. He was staring at me lazily, his enchanting grey eyes heavy like he was tired, even though he hadn't slept like I had. I squinted at him, curious.

"What's that look?" I asked, nodding towards him.

He laughed softly, shaking his head. "Could be a few things, I guess."

"Peaceful?" I asked.

He raised his fingers further up my waist, tracing a line over my ribs. "Mm, very."

I smiled. "Relieved?"

He laughed again and pressed his lips to my shoulder lightly. "You have no idea."

I faltered for a moment, focusing on the feeling of his skin against mine. I drew in a deep breath. "Happy?" I asked quietly.

His eyes found mine and immediately sensed the change in my tone. He took my face in one of his hands and kissed my cheek.

"Beyond happy." he said, holding my gaze again. I pressed my face into his hand, closing my eyes for a moment.

"Are *you* happy?" he whispered slowly.

Against my will, my head instantly went to Charlie, and dark clouds seemed to snap into existence like they'd been hiding behind the wallpaper all morning.

Charlie, laughing at a terrible joke on a slip of paper from a Christmas cracker.

Charlie, slipping me a beer behind his back at a family party, then giving me a sly wink.

Charlie, lying in his hospital bed, his green eyes closed and unable to open.

My stomach clenched painfully and I had to take a deep breath to steady myself.

I didn't deserve to be happy.

He held me gently in his hands, quiet and patient. Grey eyes swept over me and I felt him sense my hesitation. There was nothing impatient in his gaze at all, no expectation. Just *care*.

Maybe I didn't deserve to be. But I was.

I couldn't speak, so instead I just nodded.

His eyes lit up with emotion and he smiled at me with soft delight.

I smiled, turning my head into his hand shyly. To my surprise, as I held his wrist between my fingers, I felt a small ridge at the base of his palm. I turned to look at it clearer, twisting myself in place.

"What?" He asked curiously, unaware of what I'd found.

I brought his translucent hand closer to my face, peering at the mark. It was silvery-white, even in shadow and when I ran my fingertip across it again, I realised exactly what it was.

"A scar." I murmured, glancing up to him.

He was frowning, inspecting the line on his hand more closely now. "I didn't even notice."

"Something happened, while you were alive." I said slowly, "To cause that."

He nodded absentmindedly, still staring at the scar. "Probably the only evidence I'll get to have, of that life." he whispered, more to himself than to me.

Though he hadn't meant it to, something deep inside

me shattered at his words and I felt the sting of tears in my eyes. Needing to comfort him, I took his hand from him and pulled it towards me, pressing my lips to where the scar was.

Before I knew what was happening, my eyes were closed and I was somewhere else entirely.

BOTH

The sun streamed through gaps in the tree's branches up ahead, like it was fighting for space to touch the ground. Leaves danced on the gentle breeze and the sounds of the town were far away from us. We sat on the dry grass, where daisies popped their heads up shyly, dotted around us.

A teenage boy with olive skin, grey eyes and wildly dark hair was grinning at us, knelt at the base of a nearby tree trunk. When we turned our head around, the countryside seemed to go on for miles and all that could be seen apart from the summer's blessings was an old, ornate tower. Its red bricks seemed to be soaking in the warmth of the sun and the balcony on the top was painted a very pale blue.

We turned our head back to the boy, who was now faced away from us, close up against the tree's bark, fiddling with something.

"What you doing?" We heard a young boy's voice ask, echoing in our ears like it was bouncing off the walls of our minds.

The teenager sitting at the base of the tree turned to us again and we noticed a small, red Swiss-Army knife in the boy's hand. He fixed us with another cheeky grin and gestured to the bark of the tree behind him.

"Carving my name in the bark! I reckon it'll stay there for hundreds of years, unless they chop it down." The sunlight caught his eyes and made them seem light and child-like. "Come see!"

We shuffled over to the base of the tree, inspecting the boy's crude penmanship carved into the tree. In jagged capitals, were the letters 'LEO JACO'.

We nodded, then laughed a little. "You still need the B and S at the end."

The olive-skinned boy rolled his eyes, turning back to the tree. "Yeah, yeah. Hang on, I'm nearly done."

After the boy was done, he leant back and squinted his eyes at the trunk of the tree comically.

"Not bad!" he said gleefully, then turned to us. "Alright, your go!"

He handed the knife to us and we crawled closer to where he had sat, at the base of the tree. Gripping the knife in our left hand, we pressed the end of the blade against the bark. But our hands were hot and slick from the heat of the sun and when we pushed against the ridge, the blade disappeared into our closed fist, then dropped to the floor.

"Ow!" We called out instinctively, as a small stinging pain made itself known at the base of our palm.

The other boy looked at us with concern, scrambling to see the damage. We held our palm out in front of him and a small trail of blood dripped onto the grass.

"Shit," The other boy said, "that must hurt–"

HIM

Before the boy could finish his sentence, I was back in bed with Anna again, chest heaving with panic and confusion. When I looked at her, she was the same as me, green eyes wider than I'd ever seen them, completely stunned.

"Did you–" I croaked before swallowing deeply and trying again, "Did you see all that?"

"Yeah," Anna replied, shaking her head, "but it was like I was actually *there*. I could feel everything! The sun, the– the breeze, the grass underneath me. How is that..."

I lifted my arm towards me and held my palm open in front of us both, like I had done only moments ago in that field with the young boy. The silver line seemed to shine up towards us from the base and when I ran my finger across it, water pooled in my eyes for a moment.

"It was a memory." I said quietly, and Anna's eyes were fixed on my palm too. "A real one, from how I got the scar. We both saw it, when you kissed it."

We were silent for a moment, digesting everything.

"*How* is that possible?" Anna cried loudly and in spite of myself, I barked out a laugh.

"Maybe we should just stop asking how," I said, catching her eyes with mine and holding them for a moment, "it just happened."

She nodded and I smiled at how hard I could tell her brain was still working to attempt to make sense of it all. I wish I could have explained to her that she would never make sense of it all, but knew she would never listen. Anna was stubborn and logical.

"So that boy..." she started, then trailed off, looking at me.

"He must've been my friend, at some point." I

whispered, something weighing on my chest slightly.

"Not even that long ago!" Anna replied softly, "I mean, he looked younger than you do now, but not by *that* much. It could have been a few years ago, even. Do you–"

I shook my head, cutting her off before she could finish. "I don't remember him." I sighed heavily and she began stroking her fingers through my hair gently, "I still don't remember any of it. It's like it was another life completely. Like a stranger's memories."

To my surprise, Anna sat up and moved to sit opposite me, cradling my face in her hands. She smiled and the room seemed to lighten by at least two shades.

"But they weren't a stranger's memories. They were *yours*."

Her green eyes held mine and I nodded. Before long, her eyebrows furrowed again, that tireless mind at work once again.

"So, that boy's name was Leo…"

"Jacobs," I finished for her, "that's what he carved into the tree, at least. But I never saw my name, I didn't get to carve it."

Anna's face was lighting up more and more by the second. "It doesn't matter! We know his name and he knew you, however long ago it was!"

I considered her words for a moment, then began to shake my head, a little reluctantly.

"Okay, but how do we find the *right* Leo Jacobs?" I asked. She tilted her head to the side adorably and I could almost see the cogs in her mind clicking together again.

"Was there anything else in the memory that could be a clue?" Anna whispered, more to herself than to me.

I closed my eyes for a moment, going over all the details of the strange vision, trying to recall even the smallest of them.

"The tower!" I said suddenly and her head snapped towards me in surprise. Realisation dawned on her and she began nodding slowly.

"Yes! If we find where the tower is…"

Quicker than I'd ever seen her move, she launched herself across the room and grabbed her laptop from her desk, then plopped back down on the bed with it ungracefully. I couldn't help but let out a small laugh, to which she responded with a small, mock-glare.

"Okay, so…" she began, all business, starting her laptop and opening Google, "what did the tower look like? Definitely old, I'd say."

I tried my best to picture the tower in my mind again, wishing that I'd spent more time inspecting it in the memory. "Might've been Victorian, I think."

Anna started typing and I let myself fall back into the memory. The red brick, crescent shaped windows going vertically up the tower and the large, rounded blue structure on top, raised and somehow *hollow-like*, almost like…

"A water tower." I whispered, unaware of the words until I'd said them.

Anna's head turned to me, frowning.

"You think it was a water tower? Like a really old, out-of-use one?"

"I don't know why, but I think so, yeah…" I replied

slowly. Anna's eyes were still fixed on me, until she shrugged, made a face as if to say 'why not?' and began typing again.

After a few minutes searching images, her nestling back into my side so that we could both see the screen, Anna suddenly sat bolt upright and gripped the screen with both hands.

"That's the one! That's it!" she practically squealed, her eyes threatening to burst right of her head.

She moved the screen towards me and there it was. Red brick, probably about four stories, crescent windows and the pale blue water tank on top. Like it had been copied right from our minds on to the screen.

"Shit." I whispered in disbelief, "well, where is it?"

Anna took the laptop back and tapped the keypad a few times.

"Uh… it's called Appleton Tower. In… Sandringham?" She made a face. "Never heard of it… Oh, it's in Norfolk."

I kept expecting something she said to ring a bell, but still nothing came. "Apparently, it's where the huge Royal Estate is, where the Royal family have their Christmases and stuff. There's a tiny little village there, too."

Pictures of winding, cobbled streets with warm coloured buildings filled the screen. Anna clicked on and off them, trying to find everything she could.

"It's pretty." she said quietly, glancing over at me.

I couldn't say anything, so I merely nodded; smiling at her with all the warmth I had.

"I could see you growing up here, you know." she

said, gently taking my hand and running her fingers over my scar again with the lightest of touches. "You'd have to be pretty well-off, by the looks of it, but I could see that too. You speak like you're well educated."

I scoffed a little, peering down at her. "So do you!"

She dismissed me, laughing and turning back to her laptop. "Mine was self-initiated. You've got a posh-boy way about you."

Almost entirely sure that this was *not* a compliment, I glared at her, wrapping a few strands of her long dark hair around my finger and giving it a little tug. "Do not."

Anna laughed animatedly, grabbing my hand and pulling it towards her, tipping her cheek into my palm and giving me a sweet smile. Overcome by the moment, by all that we had found and the sight of her there, still sleepy and in her pyjamas but so *soft* and *happy* and *intoxicating*, I swept her into my arms, positioning her so that she was lying on my chest again, her perfect face just below mine.

Unable to stop myself as she looked at me, I traced the outline of her soft lips with one of my fingers, growing hot at the memory of what it had been like to kiss them. She blushed a little, like she could read my mind. Maybe she could.

"That could be your home." she whispered up at me, daring and gentle all at once. "We could find this guy, this Leo and maybe he could tell us where your house, or even your *family* was."

As if something a once-balanced scale set had now over-balanced, a simultaneous rising and sinking sensation struck me. She was right, of course. This was the best lead we'd had and somehow it almost seemed possible. Finding the truth. But in the pit of my stomach, I knew that with the truth, came the truth about Anna and I. The thought of facing it all at once, of her finding out and me finding out, positively made my head spin.

"We could go." she spoke again, undeterred by my silence, as she usually was. "It's only four and a half hours or so, in the car. I could drive. We could go."

I laughed sharply, entertained by her willingness and somehow not the least bit surprised. This was Anna, I was starting to realise.

"*Only* four and a half hours?" I said sarcastically, rolling my eyes for added effect. "Anna, you are supposed to be *here!* You have work, university, your friends! You can't just go off to Norfolk with no notice."

"Sure I can," she answered bluntly, unbothered by my protests, "I've barely spoken to anyone in weeks, anyway. Nobody will miss me."

I recoiled at her words like something sharp had been shoved into my breastbone. When she saw this, confusion filled her eyes and she stared at me for a moment, trying to decipher my response.

"Don't say that." I said after a while, my voice firm and steady, "Anna, don't say that, ever. People will always miss you, alright?" *No matter how much you try and push them away*, I think, but don't say aloud.

She looks a little taken aback for a minute, but then slowly nods her head, agreeing silently.

"Still," she said, softer this time, bringing her hand to trace a line from my collarbone to my jaw so that I had to hold back a shiver, "let's go. We have to go."

This time she was the one that was firm, steady. Sure of herself.

I drew in a deep breath, glancing quickly at the pictures of the charming village still loaded on her laptop screen.

"Okay." I said quietly, focusing back on her huge green eyes and offering a small smile. "We'll go."

CHAPTER 7

"I WISH I could help you pack," he said, perched on the window sill like he usually did, "but somehow I don't think I'd be much help."

As if I needed further demonstration, he attempted to pick up a dress that I'd left draped over the back of a nearby chair. The silky fabric stayed still for a moment in his hands, then fell through to the floor in a heap. I rolled my eyes as he laughed and bent over to pick up the dress from the floor, stuffing it in the overnight bag I'd nearly filled to the brim.

"You're lucky that you physically can't clear up after yourself, you know." I teased him, gesturing around the messy bedroom, "This room has been a total state since you arrived, always dropping stuff all over the floor–"

"I'm sorry–" he interrupted, ethereal eyes almost popping out of his head in indignation, "since *I* got here?! Do you know how much I've *wanted* to tidy your room?" He whipped his head around to inspect it wildly and I resisted the urge to laugh, "You are literally the messiest person I've ever met."

I couldn't help but laugh now. "Not saying much, seeing as I'm basically the *only* person you've ever met."

He shook his head at me slowly, accepting defeat with a small smile. I walked over to my wardrobe and tried to think of anything else that I might need on our impromptu trip. We'd booked a B&B to stay in for a couple of nights and although I was on a student budget, the timing was good because we were still in term-time and almost nobody would be taking a trip mid-week in late November.

"A jacket." he said, as if he'd read my mind. I frowned at him and he shrugged. "Not that I can feel it, but it looks cold out there."

When I turned back to the wardrobe, a blue and grey chequered jacket hung over to the left and I started to feel my ears ringing as I pulled it out. The inside layer was fluffy, so it was exceptionally warm, but still ran a few sizes too big on me. It wasn't made for my dainty frame, but for wider shoulders, kind eyes and a big goofy smile. I pulled it towards me for a moment, taking in its smell. Warm oranges. Like summer, wrapped up in a winter coat.

"I was always nagging him to give me this," I murmured to nobody in particular. When I looked up, I saw him looking at me anyway, softness in his silver eyes.

"Why don't you bring it?" he replied gently, "It definitely looks warm."

I shook my head, pushing the jacket back into the wardrobe hurriedly. Taking a couple of deep breaths, I forced the feeling of panic rising in my chest back down. I'd already touched it for too long – any longer and it might lose the smell of him and start picking up my scent instead.

Across the room from me, my phone began ringing, nearly making me jump out of my skin. Happy to ignore it completely, I walked about the room, trying to pull my mind back into a state of organisation again. Out of the corner of my eye, I saw him stand and peer over to where my phone lay, face up and trilling far too loudly.

He cleared his throat a little awkwardly. "Uh, it's your dad."

I shook my head, not looking at him. "He'll leave a voicemail." *He always does.*

"Anna, I've only seen you speak to your parents like, *twice* in the last month. Don't you think–"

Something snapped. "No." I said, looking up at him quickly, pleading with my eyes for him to stop speaking. I sighed heavily, hanging my head back for a moment. "It's *okay*, he'll leave a voicemail. I'll listen to it later. I'll finish packing, have some food and we can set off this afternoon."

I was lying. Though my dad had left nearly twenty messages on my phone over the last few weeks, I hadn't listened to a single one of them. They stacked up in my notifications bar and I merely dismissed them periodically, barely even tempted to listen. Each time I swallowed the shame and brushed off the guilt like it was nothing, lying to myself.

He was shaking his head, but I could sense I'd been firm enough for him to let it go, at least for now. I tried to concentrate on packing for the rest of the morning, ignoring the tugging feeling in the pit of my stomach.

By the time I was packed up and ready to go, the sun had passed its peak in the sky and the crispness of the morning had dissipated from the air. I could tell that his nerves were building because he could barely sit still all morning, entirely distracted by nothing at all. He would plop himself down on a surface, stand up only seconds later, walk a few paces, then sit somewhere else in a huff. Run his hands through his draping, illusive hair, then fiddle with his hands over and over.

He barely noticed when, as he sat on the kitchen counter, almost blending into the grey of the tiles behind him, I hoisted myself up to sit next to him. I ran a hand over his arm, relishing in the silk feeling of his skin against mine and he turned his head to me finally, as if he'd only just noticed I was there. Upon looking at me, his face softened slightly. Warmth and a hint of comfort entered his eyes and he smiled a small smile reserved only for me.

"Shall we go?" I said quietly, my face only centimetres from his. His eyes flitted between mine and my lips.

"In a minute." he murmured quietly and leaned forward to touch our lips together before I could even think about what was happening.

The tugging at my stomach lessened and heat seemed to spread all the way up my spine as I curved myself into him without thinking, coming alive under his touch. I gave a small moan of protest when he pulled away and he let out a breathy laugh. Somehow there was fire in his grey eyes.

"Come on," he said, sliding off the counter and holding his hand out for me. "Let's go."

With the car packed up and ready to go, I typed 'Sandringham' into the navigation system and he laughed when he saw how long the line between here and there was.

"Going to be a long drive." he said, looking strangely out of place in the passenger seat of my little car in broad daylight. I shook my head, peering into my mirrors to check the coast was clear before I started reversing.

"Yeah, we might have to stop at some point – SHIT!"

I braked hard and the car lurched a bit, making me jolt forward in my seat. A white van had pulled up behind us, blocking us in the driveway. I waited for a moment for the person to drive on, but instead the driver's door opened and someone got out, slamming it closed behind them.

Oh God.

"What the hell is this guy doing?" he asked beside me, craning his head around so that he could get a better view of the man striding towards us. "Oh shit, is that your–"

"Yep." I interrupted.

My dad was only a few feet from my door now and I sighed heavily before swivelling my head around.

"He can't see you, right? So just stay here for a second, I'll handle it."

"Anna–" he tried, but I wasn't listening – too busy opening my car door and stepping out.

My dad stood tall in front of me like he always had, strong and broad and bear-like. His beard had grown a little since I'd last seen him and it looked a bit unkempt now, but he still looked handsome in a messy sort of way, like he always did. He wore his usual dark jeans, workman's boots and a black jacket that had seen better days. Arms crossed on his chest and a stern look on his face, only his eyes gave him away. He looked concerned.

"Hi Dad!" I said a little falsely, plastering on a smile, "you know, you're kind of blocking me in."

He shook his head in utter disbelief. "Yeah, that was kinda deliberate, Anna. Figured you'd just drive off, otherwise."

"What?" I replied, feigning innocence, "I'm not sure why you're here, but I'm literally just on my way out dad, so could we do this another time? I can call you tonight, maybe?"

He scoffed at this, seeing right through my lie. I probably deserved that. "No, you won't! You haven't spoken to me for *weeks*, Anna. I've called you *so* many times. Eventually I decided that the only way I was actually going to *talk* to you was to come down and *hijack* you, like a madman!" His face was reddening with irritation now and he had begun tapping his boot on the ground distractedly.

"I've been busy with–"

"Bullshit, Anna!" he interrupted, not shouting exactly, but not far from it, "I called the University. I know you haven't been going to classes. I called your *mum* and I know you're speaking to *her*." He reared his head back a little, his cheeks pinched with anger, "About once in a blue moon, mind you, but it's still better than what I get, for God's sake. What the hell is going on, Anna?"

I began to shift uncomfortably, the sound of his voice bouncing around my head and making tears prick in my eyes. Unable to look directly at him, I kept my eyes fixed on his shoulder.

"Sorry, dad." Was all I could say.

"What have I *done*, love? Have I done something?" His eyes were all softness now, glassy and warm and mournful. I tried to ignore the dragging feeling in my chest. He took a couple of steps back and shook his head slightly. "You know, everything with me and your mum, it wasn't all me. Maybe you blame me, I don't know, you think I haven't been strong enough, since Charlie. But trust me, An, *I tried–*"

"*Dad.*" I said, stopping him before his words had the chance to break me. "It's not that, I swear, I just– I'm sorry I've been shit, okay? But I have somewhere to be right now."

"*Where?*" His head whipped around, as though he'd only just noticed my car sitting there, the engine still on. Staring through the window, he noticed my overnight bag. "Where the hell are you even going? Anna, just come *home* for a bit, please."

I shook my head firmly, my eyes squeezed so tightly shut that it was beginning to hurt.

"*Home?*" I half-laughed, the tears pooling in my eyes unstoppably now. "Home to *what?*"

Dad reeled back a little at this and I could see my words had hurt him. The fire was subsiding in me now and exhaustion was creeping in. It was taking everything inside me not to cry every time I looked at him.

"Anna–" he started softly, but I didn't let him finish.

"Dad, I'm really sorry, alright? But I have to go. I'll call you, I swear, but I really can't do this right now. I love you, okay?"

He shook his head defeatedly, the pain in his eyes

prominent and piercing right through me. I looked away, unable to face him any longer. I felt him fix me with a stare for a moment, then turn back towards his van and start walking away.

"We all miss him, you know!" he called out, without looking at me, "Doesn't mean we have to do it on our own."

Having blown a hole in my chest, he hoisted himself back up into his van and drove off, catching my eyes with his one last time on his way past.

HIM

I'd never known Anna to be so quiet. The roads seemed to slip by us as she drove in silence and I considered for a while what to say. Her usually pale cheeks were slightly flushed and her eyes were darkened in thought, a hard crease in between her brows.

"Anna, your dad..." I tried after a while, not knowing where exactly the sentence was going.

She shook her head slightly as though dismissing me, but I saw her eyes soften a little. Turning the wheel in her hands, she kept her sights on the road.

"I don't want to talk about it." she said quietly.

I paused for a moment, then tried again.

"I know." I said tentatively. "But I know you don't feel good about what just happened."

Her head snapped towards me. "Of course I don't!" she exclaimed, her voice louder now. "I can't believe he just *ambushed* me like that, literally no notice at all"

"Well," I countered awkwardly, "he did call, you just didn't answer."

"Okay! So he called." She rolled her eyes, then fixed them back on the road. "But you would've thought the fact that I didn't *answer* might've clued him into the fact that I *don't want to see him.*"

"But *why?*" I asked, before I could stop myself. I'm sure she could feel me staring at her, but I didn't care. "Why don't you want to see your dad? Is it really because of what happened between him and your mum, because..."

She exhaled shakily and I shut up.

"*Obviously* it's not that." Her words were harsh but her voice held no malice. "I'm not a kid, I know that everything was too hard for them. I knew from the minute Charlie was gone that it would tear them apart."

Somehow, I didn't doubt this. Anna was extremely intuitive and it didn't surprise me that she would have been able to predict the rift that would appear between her parents. I tilted my head a little, but she still wouldn't meet my eyes.

"So then, why...?"

Anna's eyes filled with tears suddenly and I cursed myself inwardly for pressing the matter. I was about to tell her to forget about it, that it wasn't my place to ask, when she started shaking her head.

"He's *so* like him." she whispered, her voice wavering as she did. As soon as the words left her mouth, everything seemed to click into place.

"Like Charlie?" I asked, when it looked like she might not say any more.

She was sniffling now, eyes still fixed on the road ahead. Without thinking, I reached out and placed my silvery hand on her arm and stroked a line up and down it.

"Yeah," she said after a while, "not just how he looks, too. Charlie *loved* dad so much, basically moulded himself to be like him. They talked the same way, told the same kind of jokes. Charlie even moved like my dad. And now..."

"Now when you see your dad..." The idea was rolling around in my head, making my chest ache as I looked at her. Beautiful, strong Anna, who couldn't even look at her dad without seeing her lost brother. Her best friend.

Tears were rolling down her cheeks freely now and she pulled the car over to stop safely at the side of the road. I pulled her closer to me so that her head rested on my chest, firm and warm.

"I know it's horrible. I'm horrible. I'm the worst daughter–"

"You're *not*, Anna. Stop it. You're grieving and–"

"But he's grieving too!" she sobbed into me and I ran my fingers through her hair. "He lost Charlie too and his wife. Now he just has me and I can't even *see him* without feeling like I'm drowning." Her voice cracked on the last syllable and I closed my arms around her tighter, as if I could fend her sadness myself. "I've failed him."

I couldn't take it anymore and pulled away from her so that she was looking directly at me. Her face was wet with tears and I could see my eerie reflection in her eyes when she looked at mine, shaken and unsure.

"You *aren't* failing him, Anna. You aren't failing anyone." I said steadily, trying to drive the point home with sincerity. "It isn't your responsibility to hold your parents up right now. All you can do is try and hold yourself up and *let them try and hold you up too.*"

She tried to look away, dismissing my words. But I held her chin in my hand, making sure her eyes didn't leave mine.

"Your dad doesn't want you to be alone. You shouldn't be alone, not ever. When you can, you should let him back in." I heaved a sigh and wiped a tear away from her cheek. "You loved Charlie so much. And as much as your dad reminds you of him and that hurts, as long as you have him, Charlie is never really gone."

She shook her head again, looking down to her lap.

"I don't think I can – not right now, I..." she trailed off and I took her hand in mine.

"It doesn't have to be now." I said softly and she looked back up to me again. "But one day, I think you'll be glad to have someone that reminds you so much of him."

My heart soared when the corners of her lips turned up a little.

"I hope so." she said quietly, squeezing my hands tightly in hers.

It was the saddest smile I'd ever seen. But it was a smile.

We had a moment of quiet before she turned the engine back on. She leaned into me, thanking me silently and I pressed a kiss to her forehead. She hummed in appreciation and my breath caught in my chest.

This is what I'm here for, I thought to myself as Anna pulled away from the side of the road, putting us back on our route again.

For her.

ANNA

The drive was long, but I didn't mind.

For a while we were quiet and I felt a little bit embarrassed about how everything had happened earlier. I'd never wanted him to see that side of me, the side that could dismiss my dad when all he was trying to do was show me kindness. The harsh side.

But it hadn't changed anything. He hadn't looked at me differently at all. I hadn't scared him, only made him want to care for me that much more. When I'd been hard and cold, he'd pulled me closer to him and filled me with warmth again. He'd told me I was wrong, but was gentle and kind about it. And the pain had lessened.

I could get used to that.

After I let go of whatever shame I felt about the situation, the journey actually became sort of fun. We talked on and on about pointless things, trivial things. I told him more about Hannah and Samantha and I loved the way he laughed at the stories of us getting into trouble together.

"So, why aren't they around so much anymore?" he asked carefully, his fingers tracing along mine on the gearstick.

"Hannah was already studying in France when everything happened with Charlie. She came back for the funeral, which was sweet." I smiled a little at the memory of her turning up at our doorstep, in a simple black dress and a little teddy bear in her hands.

She'd pulled me into the tightest hug I'd ever had and I'd thought for a minute she might actually crush my ribs. "We've been friends for a long time. It was really nice having her there."

He smiled too. "And what about Samantha?"

I sighed, shaking my head a little bit. "Things with Sam are trickier. She's been with her boyfriend for a while and she's always stayed with him a lot, which was always so nice. I was always happy to see her so happy with someone."

He nodded, understanding. "But...?"

"I don't know..." I said, trying to find the right words. "Sam's such an empathetic person. Sometimes I think that when she sees me in pain, she finds it too hard to ignore. It makes her awkward and I can tell that she doesn't know what to say to me. I know she just wants to help, but..."

"She doesn't know how?" he asked, deep in thought. I nodded.

"And I don't know how either. I don't want to give her instructions about what I need, because I don't even know myself. So we end up just avoiding any real subjects, just small-talking I guess." I shrugged, not knowing what else to say.

"And that's made you less close to each other." He was nodding, considering my words like they were a puzzle to figure out.

"Yeah," I said quietly, "I guess you're not really friends if you don't talk about what's actually going on with you. You're sort of just, acquaintances."

He looked at me then, questions behind his eyes.

"Do you miss having them around?" he asked gently.

I considered his question. There were a few times where I'd been alone in the house and wished that they were there, for some company. But compared to the bottomless hole that appeared whenever I thought of Charlie, it was miniscule. Nothing.

"I miss how things used to be, sometimes." I shrugged and caught his eyes for a moment. "But friends come and go."

He was quiet for a moment before he spoke. With the light streaming in through the window, he looked entirely weightless and mystical in the seat next to me. He smiled at me with so much care, then turned back to the road.

"They don't have to." he said after a while, contemplative, like he always was.

I played some of the music I liked for a bit and he laughed at my terrible singing, offbeat and offkey.

"God, you're the literally the worst singer that's ever lived." he said, between fits of laughter.

I tried to fake offence but couldn't manage it and laughed even harder.

"I actually took singing lessons when I was a kid!" I shouted over the music. His silvery eyes nearly popped out of his head.

"You're *joking*." he said, covering his mouth with his hand to stop himself from laughing. "And it didn't stick?"

I shook my head, grinning. "Too much natural talent. They didn't know what to do with it all."

He laughed and something jumped in my chest, happy and light.

The sun had begun to set, and the orange hues

caught the shape of him like a watercolour painting. He was so beautiful this way, beside me, the sound of his voice calm and melodious, filling the car and soothing my mind like cool water on a burn. I couldn't help but keep glancing over at him and had to remind myself multiple times to keep my eyes on the road.

"I love looking at you." he said suddenly, while I was trying to read the signs on the side of the road in the dwindling light.

When I turned to him, I could barely speak for the look in his eyes. I couldn't tell exactly what it was, but it seemed to stop everything inside me from functioning. A little scared of his sincerity, I couldn't meet his eyes for long.

I turned back to the road. "I was just thinking the same about you."

HIM

The drive was long, but I didn't mind.

By the time we got to Sandringham, all the natural daylight had almost gone. Anna seemed invigorated by the success of the journey and when we checked into the bed and breakfast she was beaming secretly at me while the receptionist gave her our key.

"We got here in one piece!" she said happily, plopping down on the bed heavily and spreading her limbs out like she was making a snow angel.

I laughed a little, happy to see her happy after the day's events. Though I was glad to have arrived finally. The weight of our purpose there had seemed to settle on my shoulders uncomfortably and I could feel nerves twisting in my stomach, making me a little uneasy. I strolled about the room for a moment, inspecting the view from the bay windows.

"It's beautiful here." I said quietly. The windows looked out onto a meadow which seemed to stretch for miles and enormous trees that were losing their leaves shook gently in the wind, waving to me in the twilight.

Anna hummed in agreement, sitting up straight on the bed. The lamplight was warm on her face, bringing a glow to her usually pale skin. Her dark eyelashes cast a shadow below her eyes, she was smiling at me slightly.

She was the most beautiful thing I'd ever seen.

"What are you thinking?" she asked. I smiled at her, shaking my head a little.

"Just that I can't believe we're really here. That we're really doing this."

My head was spinning slightly when I came to sit next to her on the bed. She turned to me and brought her hand to my face, holding it.

"Are you nervous?" she asked, her eyes flitting between my eyes and my lips. The world seemed to tilt on it's axis with her there beside me, touching me so gently, care in her eyes.

"No." I said honestly. Because there were no nerves that could penetrate the warmth that she had shrouded me in. "Not right now."

She smiled and the light touched her eyes, making them bright and clear. "We could find out who you are, who you were." Anna moved her fingers through my hair. "I can't wait to know you completely."

Something about what she said caught me off guard

and suddenly the nerves started to settle in again. What if who I was wasn't good enough? What if I was a person who wasn't good and didn't deserve someone like Anna to care about me? What if this was a mistake?

"What if we don't like who I was?" I used *we* instead of *you* to protect myself, not wanting to give too much away as to what I was really thinking.

She smiled, as if she knew what I'd really meant. "Impossible. How could you be so wonderful in death if you hadn't been in life?"

Without even knowing, she'd said exactly what I'd needed her to. Pushing my anxiety to the side, I placed my hands on her waist and moved her over toward me, so that she was almost sat entirely on my lap. She laughed softly, then stopped when she saw how I was looking at her. Like I wasn't letting her go anywhere. Like I couldn't. Like nothing on earth could stop me from touching her. If the room had been torn apart by an earthquake in that moment, she would have stayed right there, on my lap, with me looking at her the same way.

"What's that look?" she whispered, like she was scared to hear the answer.

I opened my mouth to answer her, but decided better of it and pulled her even closer to me instead. With my hands in her hair, I brought her lips down to mine quickly and we crashed together like two waves meeting. I was out of breath before I even registered that I didn't *need* to breathe. I couldn't stop moving my fingers across her skin, so warm and soft. Spreading them out across her back, I crushed her body to mine and she whined a little. I couldn't believe how amazing she tasted. I couldn't get enough of her like that, hot and sweet and on my lap, wanting me. But–

"Okay, okay," I gasped, pulling away from her. "We've got to stop."

Her face was flushed and stunning and her eyes were dark with want and it was like a dream – her, sat there, tugging at me like she couldn't have me close enough and I'd stopped it. *I'd stopped it*. Was I crazy?!

"No, no we don't–" she started, searching my eyes for answers, "I want–"

I stopped her because I had to. Because I couldn't hear her say that she wanted me. It would break my paper-thin resolve in a second and feeling her there, pleading with me with her eyes was enough to make me want to throw away all my restraint anyway and bring her lips back to mine again.

"Anna, it's been a crazy day." I half-laughed, trying to lighten the mood. "I'm betting what we *really* want is some sleep. We have a big day tomorrow, you know..." I rubbed the back of my neck anxiously, "soul-searching and stuff."

She frowned for a moment, then nodded and retreated back to her side of the bed. For a moment I considered going back on everything I'd just said, saying *fuck it* and pulling her back to me. But I knew I couldn't. It wasn't right to be with her like this. Not yet, anyway.

When we got under the covers and turned out the lights, darkness settled in and Anna nestled up beside me. I could feel her warmth through her clothes. Everything seemed to make a little bit more sense with her there next to me, tying me down to the earth with her.

I took her hand in mine and rubbed it lightly, looking at her with all the sincerity I could muster. "Hey, I'm *so* glad that you're here with me. I couldn't be here without you." If only she knew how true that really was.

But she simply smiled and pressed a sweet kiss to my cheek.

"No, you couldn't." she said sleepily, her head resting on my chest. "You can't drive."

CHAPTER 8

ANNA

WHEN THE SUN rose the next morning, I was ready for it. Ready for the day and ready for answers.

I watched him carefully as I went through my morning routine, stretching while he lay still on the bed next to me, shimmering slightly in the stray rays of light escaping through the curtains. When I rested my hand on his shoulder and let my warmth flow through him, he looked up to me with an almost unreadable smile.

"You ready?" I asked, simply.

Still with that sad smile, he took my hand and pressed it to his lips. A shiver went from my fingertips all the way up my arm and down to the base of my spine.

"No." he laughed quietly, but sat up and got out of the bed all the same.

An hour and a half later, we were walking towards the supposed house of his supposed former friend.

"This is the stupidest plan I've *ever* heard, Anna." he said loudly, "There is *no way* you're doing this."

I whipped around to face him, sending my scarf over my shoulder at the same time, protecting myself from the biting wind.

"First of all, this plan isn't *stupid*, okay? It's..." I tipped on the balls of my feet while I considered what might be the best word, "ill-advised, maybe, but that's it. Second of all, I don't see *any* other way to do this, short of me explaining that the *amnesiac ghost* of his possible friend is *haunting me.*"

"Anna–"

"And I can promise you that this little dynamic," I pointed wildly between the two of us, "is not going to be so charming and cute once this guy has me *sectioned*, okay?"

"Anna it's not going to work, okay."

"Do you have a better idea?" I half shouted, half whispered back to him.

He paused for a moment, light and airy by my side on the cobbled street, considering my words. Then, his eyes full of defeat, he just shook his head.

"He's going to think you're a psycho." he half-laughed, shaking his head.

I tried to stifle a laugh as an old lady and her dog walked past. "Well apparently I see dead people, so he wouldn't be too far off."

When we arrived at the house, we stood silently for a moment outside of the front door. It was painted a rich plum colour, complimenting the warm brick walls. An old-fashioned metal doorbell hung above the doorframe, with a small chain to pull to ring it.

I blew out a puff of air and glanced at him. He gave me an uneasy look back, but grabbed my hand as if to say *I'm here. I'm in.*

"How are your acting skills?" he whispered to me, forgetting that he didn't need to.

I stared at the door. "I took drama for GCSE."

He grinned and nodded, looking down at me with a little more hope.

"And?" he prompted me.

I inhaled sharply. "Had a panic attack in the middle of my monologue, then fainted on one of the other actors and knocked them off the back of the stage."

He nodded, the hope gone from his expression and a look of resignation on his face again. Then, against all my expectations, he let out a laugh.

"Fuck it. Ring the bell, lets do this." he said quietly, giving my hand a little squeeze.

So, I rang the bell.

HIM

I'm not sure how many moments we stood at that door, waiting for it to open. For me, a whole lifetime passed.

When it finally clicked and swung open, I found myself resisting the urge to bolt. To run down the street as fast as I could, away from all of it. What the hell were we even *doing*? But Anna held my hand and kept my feet steady on the ground. I was not going anywhere without her.

The man who opened the door was not Leo Jacobs, he was far too old, but the olive skin seemed to pull some familiarity to the young boy in the memory. He gave Anna a little confused smile, towering over her small frame like a big friendly bear.

"I'm sorry sir, but is there a Leo Jacobs who lives here?" Anna said in her talking-to-a-stranger-voice, simpering and unassuming. I couldn't help but grin at how *un*Anna it sounded.

"There is yeah, are you one of Leo's friends?" The guy asked, smiling at her. "I don't remember seeing you around before."

Anna smiled back, her huge green eyes sparkling with sincerity. "I'm more like a friend of a friend, really. Is Leo about?"

"Sure, yeah. Come in." The man said, pushing the door wide for her to enter through. Before he could shut the door behind her, I quickly slipped through the space in between and Anna pretended not to notice.

Standing in the hallway, it all felt a little strange, being in somebody else's house when they couldn't even *see* me. Didn't even know I was there. The man looked right through me when he spoke to Anna, none the wiser. Something ached in my chest, but I tried my hardest to ignore it.

"I think Leo's upstairs, studying in his room. Or pretending to study." The man laughed in a friendly way and Anna laughed too. "Can I get you a drink of water, or anything…"

"It's Emily," Anna lied seamlessly, "and no, I'm okay thank you! Is it okay if I go up to see Leo?"

The guy was backing away already, nodding towards Anna. "Of course, yeah. Nice to meet you, Emily."

Before I knew it, we were walking up the two flights of carpeted stairs towards Leo's bedroom.

"So far so good." Anna whispered to me as we climbed, looking around at the family pictures around her as she walked.

"Why'd you lie about your name?" I whispered back. Even though nobody would be able to hear me speak, the feeling of intruding on this family home made me more cautious than I normally would be.

Anna grimaced. "Don't know, just came out."

I couldn't help but laugh, shaking my head at her.

When we got to Leo's bedroom door, I felt the breath inside me falter a little. Anna knocked.

"Leo?" she called out.

There was some confused mumbling from the other side of the door and then it swung open.

Leo was tall and slightly lanky, with arms and legs that seemed only a little too long for his body. He had the darkest hair I'd ever seen on a guy before, jet black and sticking out in funny directions, like it could never be tamed. His skin was the same olive colour as his dad's was, the same colour as in the memory. Though he had changed a lot since whenever the memory had been, when his light grey eyes passed over Anna, frowning in confusion, I knew it was the same boy. He'd just grown a bit.

"Uh, hi," he said, his eyes flitting about a bit in confusion. "I'm sorry, do we–"

"No, sorry, hi." Anna interrupted, a little flustered, "We don't know each other, my name's Emily though."

In spite of his bewilderment, Leo seemed friendly and gave Anna a small smile in greeting.

"I know this is a bit weird, but um," Anna started and I could feel her act slipping a little bit, "I was wondering whether I could talk to you. About someone that you know."

Leo seemed to consider the situation for a moment and I could almost see the cogs going around in his head. Strange, pretty girl at his door. He doesn't know her, but she seems relatively sane. And he's definitely intrigued. She's only small, how much of a risk could it be, really?

"Sure, why not?" he said eventually, holding the door open wide for her, mirroring the way his father had done earlier.

I grinned down at Anna and she gave me a secretive smile as Leo pulled up a stool for her to sit on, opposite him.

Leo had quite a room set up, with skylights in his ceiling and the white walls of his bedroom, I'm sure I was barely visible to Anna for blending in. She pretended not to notice me as I sat beside her on the stool, my leg pressed up against hers. I fought the urge to press my lips gently to her temple, as I knew I couldn't distract her. Her eyes were fixed on Leo now and I could tell that she seemed a little nervous.

"So… What exactly did you want to talk about?" Leo started, an intrigued and slightly uncomfortable tone to his voice.

Anna laughed a little, shaking her head. "It's going to sound a little crazy so, uh, bear with me, but um…" I stroked a line down her arm and she smiled a small smile, a smile for me, then continued talking, "For the past year or so, I've been talking to a guy who lives in this village. I live sort of far away from here, uh… Cornwall, actually."

I resisted the urge to laugh by pressing my non-existent feet into the floor as hard as I could. She *literally* couldn't have gone any further away on the map if she'd tried.

But Leo was nodding, a more relaxed look on his face now that things were being attempted to be explained.

"And um, we've actually been speaking through letters, the whole time." She sent a small smile to Leo, attempting to look shy. "I'm a little bit introverted, really, so I thought it would be a nice way to keep up a friendship, you know? So I went on one of those websites and they matched me up with him. We've been writing to each other ever since. But we always stayed anonymous."

Leo looked even more puzzled now, his dark eyebrows furrowed tightly, grey eyes fixed on Anna's green ones.

"Uh, I'm really sorry Emily, but I don't write letters or anything, really–"

Immediately, Anna began laughing good-naturedly, which caused Leo to reel back a little.

"No, no, don't worry. I'm not asking if you're him!"

Leo grinned in relief, sitting back in his chair, a little more relaxed.

"Good, okay." he sighed. "So, why *are* you here speaking to me, then?"

Anna sighed, looking to her lap for a moment, playing the part. I almost whistled because I was so impressed with her performance, but I knew that would put her off.

"Well, I haven't heard from him in a few months now. It was like he just disappeared completely! I'm visiting the Royal Grounds with my family this weekend and when I found out that the little village he was from was just down the road from where we were, it seemed like the perfect time to come and see him."

Leo was nodding slowly, his eyes a little wider now.

"Right, but… you don't know who he is?"

Anna shook her head, her gorgeous eyes wider than they ever had been.

"Not his name, no. But I did know yours. He mentioned you a couple of times in his letters, saying that he was hanging out with you that week. Or he'd tell me a memory of you guys, when he would talk about being a kid."

Anna was cautious with her words, not wanting to freak Leo out. She was doing well, it seemed. The guy definitely looked a bit confused, but at least he wasn't looking at her like she was a crazy stalker. Only Anna could make half-stalking seem sweet.

"Right, so… you're saying *I* know him? I mean, if he knows me, then–"

"Right, exactly. That's what I assumed, too." Anna replied brightly, hopefully.

My breath was starting to quicken, sat there opposite this guy whom I was supposed to have shared memories with. I kept flitting my eyes over his face, trying desperately to take note of some feature, some crease in his brow that might jog my memory. I was still as a statue as he sat there, oblivious of me, deliberating. Unbeknownst to him, this boy was my guide through the darkness, sat there, deciding whether or not to turn on the light.

"I mean, without sounding like a dick, I have quite a few friends around this area. Is there anything specific that he told you that might–"

Unable to help herself from jumping at the question, Anna interrupted.

"He did tell me about this one specific time, from

when you guys were teenagers, I think?" she said quickly, leaning forward on her knees, inspecting Leo's face, "He said something about being near a water-tower around here and carving your names into a tree?"

My eyes swivelled rapidly between Anna and Leo's faces. Anna, hopeful and curious. Leo, tugging at his memory like a tightly wrapped ball of yarn with a loose thread.

"I'm sorry, I don't really remember. I spent so much time out with my friends around here, it could've been any of them."

The room seemed to be getting darker by the moment and everything that had once clicked into place threatened to fall back out again.

"He cut his hand, when he tried to carve his name. That's what he told me." Anna interrupted desperately, clutching at the last hope we had. My stomach turned over and over with her words.

Everything seemed to still in the room for a moment, once her words hung around us all. And then realisation dawned on Leo's face and without thinking, I reached out for Anna's hand, interlacing my fingers through hers. I needed her to ground me.

Leo sucked in a deep breath, then brought his hands to his face, rubbing them tiredly.

"Right, yeah… Of course, you haven't heard from him…" Leo began muttering more to himself than to Anna and I imagined my non-existent heart thrumming inconsolably in my hollow chest.

Anna, buzzing with anticipation but trying her hardest to be patient, merely pressed her lips together, before speaking quietly.

"You know who it is?" she whispered, quickly shooting me a glance. I held her eyes there for a moment, needing them.

Leo sighed heavily, his head bowed in front of him. After a moment he looked up and the sadness in his eyes nearly took the breath right out of me.

"Emily, I'm really sorry." he began eventually, his voice low with anguish, "I don't wanna tell you this, I really don't. But the guy you were writing to, I think, I think he's… gone now. That's why you haven't heard from him. I really am sorry."

When I looked to Anna, I was surprised to see real tears in her eyes, threatening to spill onto her cheeks.

"Anna, hey…" I whispered, momentarily breaking my silence. I stroked her hand with mine, but she did not look at me.

"That's…" She didn't speak for a moment, just cleared her throat and tried again. "That's really sad."

Leo nodded heavily. "I know."

"Who… Who was he?" Anna asked quietly.

Everything and nothing hung on his answer. Leo was going to say a name. It was just a name, like every person on earth had. But it was *mine. My name.*

Leo gave a small smile. "His name was Joe. Joe Brooks. He was my friend."

My chest felt tight and Anna gripped my hand as tightly as she could without arousing suspicion.

My name was Joe. My name was Joe Brooks. My name was Joe.

Anna smiled, one of her tears finding its way to her cheek as she did.

"Joe." she said softly, then laughed a little. "It suits him."

I couldn't help but laugh a little, glad to have her with me. Leo, oblivious to our little exchange, just smiled again and nodded.

"What, um…" Anna glanced at me again now and I nodded my consent. She ran her thumb over my hand comfortingly. "What happened to him?"

Leo shook his head slowly, a sad frown on his usually boyish face.

"I don't know exactly; nobody over here got all the details. It's a bit of a mystery actually."

I looked at Anna and though her head stayed faced towards Leo, her eyes met mine for a moment.

"A mystery," Anna frowned, "what do you mean?"

Leo splayed his palms out on his thighs, rubbing there distractedly. "Well, the last I ever heard from him was some time in summer, they were still abroad, in the South of France– Oh!"

He got up to stand suddenly, as if he was just remembering something. When his back was turned, Anna turned to me frantically, mouthing silently to me –

South of France?

"I don't know!" I said quietly, despite Leo not being able to hear me. "I still can't remember anything!"

Leo rooted around in what seemed to be a drawer of paperwork while Anna looked at me, wide eyed.

Posh. She mouthed to me, winking.

I laughed a little, feeling light-headed. When Leo had returned to sit with us, he was holding a small rectangular piece of card in his olive hands. Anna's eyebrows shot up.

"It's a postcard from Joe, from the beginning of the summer. Last time we spoke." He handed the postcard over to Anna and she took it quickly, leaning over to me so that I could see it.

On the front was a picturesque city, Montpellier, adorned with enormous traditional French buildings with ornate fixtures. The sun shone down on the town square and people bustled past each other to get to their appointments. It was beautiful.

With delicate fingers, Anna slowly turned over the postcard, her other hand still clasped in mine. The handwriting on the other side was written in blue ink and was a little smudged.

Leo,

Hope your summer is going good mate! Montpellier is great, but way too hot, as usual.

I mainly just sent this postcard to make you jealous, like I do every year.

Should be back in September, though my parents say they want to stay longer. Honestly, they're doing my nut in. Jean Luc says that we should just take off for a week on his Dad's boat if it gets too much. Remember the one? You got so drunk when you came over that one time, you ended up trying to climb up on the bull by the carousel. Ah, happy days.

See you when I'm back!

Joe

Anna's breath was ragged as she swept her eyes over

the writing and I could barely hold myself together.

"That's my writing…" I started, hardly knowing if it was a question or a statement.

Anna nodded silently and Leo frowned slightly, but said nothing of it.

"There's a return address…" Anna murmured quietly, running her thumb gently over the ink.

"Yeah," Leo said, making me jump a little, "His parents have a place out there, they go every year."

I couldn't take my eyes away from the postcard. The way the pen curled on the y's, the way the dots on the i's were slightly off centre. This was *me. I had written those words.*

"So, his parents, are they still out there?" Anna asked gently, her voice barely above a whisper.

Leo nodded again. "As far as I know, yeah. They definitely didn't come back to Sandringham and there was no service for Joe here, so I assumed that they just…"

Buried me there.

Suddenly the room was getting too small and this stranger was far too close to us for me to feel like I could breathe properly.

"Anna, can we go?"

Anna did a small nod to convey that she'd heard me, then went back to speaking to Leo.

"Do you mind if I take a picture of this?" she asked him, all sweetness and sincerity, "I was thinking about writing to his parents, you know, just to give my condolences."

Leo agreed with no issues and before we knew it, we were back in the hallway of the house again, Anna saying her goodbyes.

"Thank you, Leo." she said quietly, smiling at him genuinely.

When he smiled back his grey eyes lit up a little. "You're welcome. I'm sorry it wasn't better news."

After Anna had walked through the door, I stood in front of her for a moment, staring through the closing gap at Leo. Light grey eyes and a cheeky, wide smile. My *friend*.

Completely unaware of my ghostly form, he merely looked down to the carpet as he shut the door and the next moment he was gone.

A lump formed in my throat and I stared at the cobbles on the street for a moment, trying to compose myself.

Anna's arm looped around my waist and her face appeared at my side. She was smiling, but her green eyes were full of gentle care.

"Hey, you okay?" she asked softly.

I didn't know the answer.

"I'm Joe." I said quietly and her smile widened a little.

"So I heard." she said, pulling me closer to her, so that we were wrapped up in a tight hug. "Enough soul-searching for one day. Let's go for a walk."

ANNA

Joe.

Now that I thought of it, it seemed so obvious. *Of course* he was a Joe, his eyes so full of warmth, his arms always moving protectively over me, shielding me, his words so kind and sincere. He was never going to have a fancy, superficial name. He was always going to be solid, sturdy, salt of the earth. Joe.

Joe and Anna. Anna and Joe.

"What are you smiling at?" he said suddenly, glancing at me sideways, breaking me free of my thoughts.

"Hmm?" I said, startled, "Oh, nothing. It's just really pretty here."

He grinned at me, nodding and turning his head back to the lake. It was still and quiet and there was nobody around to notice us.

"Uh huh." he said and I rolled my eyes at him.

The biting cold seemed to have disappeared for a moment and the sun shone through the thin layer of cloud that it hid behind. I hummed in appreciation as the rays warmed my back and Joe looked over to me.

"What you thinking?" I asked, knowing that it was an enormous question.

He was quiet for a moment and I watched the ripples of a fallen leaf on the lake disperse outwards through him.

"That guy, Leo. He was my friend." he said simply and I nodded, pretty sure I understood where this was going.

"But you didn't remember him?" I said quietly.

He shook his head, then blew out a breath.

"I thought it would change everything. Knowing my name, who I was, but… Everything feels the same. It's like nothing has changed."

I nodded slowly, taking in his words with consideration.

"Did you think it might jog your memories and you would get them back?" I asked.

He shrugged heavily. "Not necessarily. I just thought it would be different. I thought I'd feel different, but I don't."

"And how do you feel?" I asked, curiosity getting the better of me once again.

"Well, glad to know that I at least had one friend, when I was alive." he joked.

"Ah, you were rich," I countered, bumping my shoulder against his, "he was probably just in it for the holiday house."

Joe laughed silently, nodding his head. I smiled, but something was tugging at my chest.

"How do you *actually* feel?" I said, quieter this time.

He turned to look at me, transparent and beautiful with eyes half his silver colour, half the sky's blue. Running his eyes over my face, he brought his hand up to tangle in my hair.

"Lost, still. Like none of this is real. Like you're the only thing that is."

"Why me?" I mumbled, unsure of my words.

"You're the only thing that feels real, to me."

His eyes were on mine, then on my lips. If I concentrated hard enough, I could convince myself that I could feel his breath on my face.

"I'm sorry." I said quietly, but he shook his head.

"Don't be. I'm not."

The day seemed to pass us by as if time were foreign to us. For thousands of years or mere minutes, it was just us by the edge of the lake. Joe and Anna. The dead and the living. Tangled together in ways unknown, like a piece of string that could not be unwoven.

CHAPTER 9

JOE?

THE NEXT DAY we drove home, back to the house where most of my memories were held safely. I tried my best not to stay quiet in the car – to talk to Anna whenever I felt like I could. Half of me felt like my mind had been racing ever since our conversation with Leo and the other half of me felt very still. Like water on the surface of a lake, trying to remain undisturbed.

Anna, ever the impatient, was trying her best too. I knew that my quiet was killing her, that she had a million questions that she wanted to ask, stacking up beneath the surface of her calm and kind eyes. She'd touch my hand, gentle and smile at me with a lightness that didn't quite touch her eyes.

"You okay?" She finally asked, when we were stopped at a service station so that Anna could have one of her ridiculously large coffees.

I took a deep breath in, not caring that I didn't need it, while I really considered her question.

Everything felt sort of off-kilter, now that I knew who I was. Like I was on the precipice, teetering on the edge of something that might turn everything on its head. But I couldn't quite get there. I couldn't quite reach it.

I looked at Anna, cradling her enormous, iced coffee (almost December!) in her dainty hands. Her eyes were fixed on my face, wide with curiosity and concern. And everything seemed to turn back to its original place. The ground that I walked on was flat again, safe. My feet were steady, as long as she was holding my hand.

"I have you." I said simply, bringing my hand to tangle in her long hair. "I'll always be okay."

At this, she gave me a genuine smile. Unable to stop myself any longer, I moved my hand to cup her face and brought it towards me, needing to feel her lips against mine. She smiled into the kiss slowly, like it was giving her the same sense of warmth and life as it did me. When she eventually pulled away, her cheeks were my favourite shade of pink. Anna's shade.

ANNA

He wasn't himself; I could tell. He was quieter and it barely mattered that I was smiling over at him now and then while I drove, or that he'd reach for my hand when he felt like he needed it. I could feel his thoughts and questions, running around inside the car as we approached home.

"There's another car in the drive." he said suddenly, breaking me free from my musings as we finally pulled into my road.

He was right. Samantha's white fiat was planted where my car normally sat, complete with her little monkey figurine hanging from the mirror. I could see it dangling from where we sat, quiet in the driveway.

"It's Sam's." I said, turning my head to look at him. To my surprise, instead of there being apprehension on his face like I expected, he was grinning at me.

"She's home! That's great!"

I half-laughed at him, then looked back to the house.

"I guess?" I shook my head a little, trying to get my head straight. "Well, she can't see you either, so let's just go in. We can disappear into my room for the night once I've said hello."

He looked a little doubtful at that, but nodded his head with a smile anyway.

The house was already warm when we came in through the front door and I couldn't help but smile a little. It was nice to come home to a warm house.

Normally, walking through the door, the house felt a little barren and empty and cold. But now I could feel the warmth from the radiators and smell Sam's signature peach perfume drifting pleasantly through the hallway.

When we got to the kitchen, Sam was facing away from me, stooped over the far counter, fiddling with something. With a quick glance at Joe, who was stood a few feet behind me, giving me an encouraging smile, I cleared my throat a little.

"Hey, I didn't know you were gonna be here–" I started to say, but Sam whipped around before I could finish my greeting.

I'd always been a little jealous of the way that Samantha was built – tall, lean and athletic looking. She was somehow tanned all year-round, even at this time of the year. I knew she worked hard to keep her body the shape it was – she was constantly in the gym with her boyfriend doing couples workouts, which I would rather die than ever do. I envied her tall slenderness, feeling like it gave her an elegance that I would never have. Her honey-toned highlights were framing her face beautifully and her light brown eyes lit up as soon as they saw me.

"Hi stranger!" she laughed, pulling me into a hug before I even knew what was happening.

Joe laughed a little behind us, unbeknownst to Samantha, as he stood there looking directly at her. He was probably amused by the height difference, as she nearly completely enveloped me in her hug.

When she pulled away, she was still smiling, but a little sadder this time. "I feel like I haven't seen you in *years*." She took a few strands of my hair between her fingers and looked them over. "I can't believe how long your hair is now. You're like the little mermaid."

I laughed, shaking my head. "I know, I really need to get it cut."

She shrugged good-naturedly. "I like it."

"So, what brings you back home?" I asked.

"Oh, uh, it's getting *really* cold out there, so I came back to get all my heavy winter coats so I'm not freezing my ass off every time I walk to the shop."

I heard Joe sigh a little behind me and tried to resist the urge to turn around and look at him.

"Ah, right." I nodded slowly at her and she nodded back, avoiding my eyes. She shifted her weight between her feet for a moment, then looked back to me.

"And I missed you." she blurted out, like she hadn't really meant to say it. "And Hannah, I mean, but I'm sort of used to being without her now, I guess. I really missed *you*, though." Sam sighed and leaned back on the counter for a minute. "I did try and call, a lot–"

"I know, it's my fault." I interrupted before she could

carry on, "I've been so shit with that stuff recently, keeping in touch–"

"I know." Sam said quietly, meeting my eyes. "I'm not mad or anything, I just missed you. I get it, though."

We were quiet for a moment, but it wasn't uncomfortable. I shot a glance towards Joe, who was resting against the doorframe, silent and almost luminous against the hallway lights behind him.

"I met a guy." I said, before I could stop myself.

Joe inhaled sharply behind me and Sam's jaw actually dropped, her eyes widening in shock.

"Shut the fuck up!" she nearly shouted, her mouth in a grin of pure delight. "Where?! What's his name?"

I laughed, taking a seat at one of the chairs near the counter. Sam stayed standing across the room, bouncing about on the balls of her feet like she physically couldn't contain her excitement.

"His name's Joe." I said, smiling at her. From the corner of my eye, I could see Joe in the corner, shaking his head slowly with a smile. "I met him, uh, through uni. He's in one of my classes."

I could hardly believe what I was saying myself. Was I really talking about him? Out loud? To someone *I actually knew?*

Sam was grinning at me still, her palms pressed to her cheeks in disbelief. "This is the *best* news I've ever heard. Tell me literally everything about him, please."

I grimaced slightly, scolding myself for ever bringing it up. "What do you want to know?"

Sam considered my question, frowning slightly.

"Is he good looking?" she asked quickly.

"Oh, God." Joe whispered behind me and I nearly

burst out laughing.

"Definitely." I said, smiling.

Sam squealed. "Okay, okay. Tall?"

"Be nice." Joe said quietly and I pressed my lips together.

"Tall enough." I said and Sam nodded like I'd said the right thing.

"Funny?"

"*Really* funny. Maybe even funnier than me."

"*Doubt that.*" Sam and Joe both said in unison and I laughed in delight.

"So what's wrong with him?" Sam asked, curiosity. "There's got to be something. Jason has the *worst* taste in music I've ever heard. Every time he puts his playlists on, I honestly wish I was born deaf." Joe laughed loudly, shaking his head. "So?"

The air seemed to get heavier around me at the question and suddenly my chest felt uncomfortably restricted. I couldn't look at Joe, entirely perfect, standing looking at me, waiting for me to point out his flaws.

I took a deep breath in an attempt to steady myself. "Well, he can't drive." I said and Sam pondered for a moment.

"Annoying, but not a deal breaker." she said too seriously and I smiled.

When I could finally bring myself to look at him, his eyes were already on me, warm and distant all at once.

"I think he might have some commitment issues." I said quietly, unsure of whether I'd even said it aloud. But Joe frowned, hurt touching his face.

Oblivious to our little exchange, Sam sighed and

came to sit beside me. She leaned one of her elbows up against the counter and tipped her head towards me.

"I wouldn't worry too much about that." she said, nudging my shoulder with hers.

"Why not?" I frowned.

She shrugged, letting her honey-coloured hair fall across her face. "I think you're the kind of person that people want to stick around for. If you let them."

It was quiet for a moment again. I didn't look at the almost invisible boy in the corner of the room, pulling me towards him with his eyes. Instead, I looked at Sam. She smiled at me and rubbed my forearm affectionately.

"It's really good to see you, An." Her words were so sincere that they took me by surprise and I had to remind myself to smile back at her. "Are things, you know… okay?"

I considered the question, thinking back over all that had happened since I last saw her. Skipped meals. Days in bed. Ignoring my parents' calls. Watching the birds cling to the branches of trees in the forest where we walked. Sitting by the lake while the sun shone through him.

"I have moments of okay." I said honestly, looking up at her with a humble smile, which she returned in earnest.

"Moments are better than nothing." she said, wrapping her arm around my shoulder and resting her head there for a moment. I breathed in and out, enjoying the feeling of having her close to me again.

"I have to go, Anna, I'm sorry. I've got work in a little

bit." Sam said, standing up and grabbing her phone from the counter.

I nodded. "Okay, no worries."

She stood in the doorway for a small moment, only a metre or so away from Joe, who had his eyes fixed on me.

"I'm going to be around more." she said quietly, looking down at her feet awkwardly. "I know that should have been from the beginning, really, but it was just hard to–"

"Sam," I interrupted her and her head snapped up to meet my eyes, "it's not your fault."

"No," she said sadly, shaking her head slowly, "it is, I know it is. I *wanted* to be here, I swear I did. I just–"

"Sam, seriously," I said, taking a step towards her and Joe, "it's okay. I know you wanted to. And I should have let you."

She nodded, reflecting my sad smile back to me. I laughed a bit, feeling all the tension lift from my chest.

"It's *so* nice to have you around." I said earnestly and Sam almost looked like she might burst into tears on the spot. She laughed a little raggedly, nodded and sniffled.

She called goodbye from the front door when she left, saying that she would be back for a few days the following week. When the door clicked shut, I sat for a moment on the chair she had sat at near the counter, smiling at Joe's figure in the doorway.

He took a couple of steps towards me with a small smile.

"She loves you." he said quietly and I couldn't stop the tears from gathering in my eyes, or the lump from forming in my throat.

I nodded silently, smiling through bleary eyes.

"I know." I replied, wiping a fallen tear from my cheek.

JOE?

We went walking that evening.

As far as I could tell from Anna – the pink tip of her nose, her shivering every now and then – it was freezing. Yet I walked beside her, unflinching in the biting wind, taking steps that never made a sound. The grass pressed flat under her feet when she walked upon it and bristled only slightly when I drifted through.

"What are you thinking about?" she asked quietly, looping her arm through mine while we sat on a park bench somewhere.

The light was fading fast and the outline of the trees against the sky was barely visible.

"What you said to Samantha." I said quietly, not looking at her.

I felt her nod beside me. "I don't know why I said that, I'm sorry. It just came out."

I sighed, reaching for her hand and interlacing her fingers with my ghostly ones.

"I know why you said it." I whispered, watching the silhouettes of the pine trees fade into the blackness.

The house was quiet again when we got back, but there was enough unsaid to feel as though words were bouncing from the walls.

Anna sat down on the bed and took her huge green coat off, throwing it on the floor at her feet.

I sat opposite her in her desk chair for a moment, considering what to say.

"We should talk about it." I said quietly, trying to catch her eyes.

She huffed a little, giving me a steely look. "About what?"

"About this! *Us!*" I exclaimed, gesturing between the two of us with an airy hand.

Anna threw her head back in frustration. "Why?! I don't want to talk–"

"But I need to know how you're feeling."

"*Oh my God.*" she groaned, putting her head in her hands.

I took a deep breath, trying to keep my head straight. "Anna, I can't read your mind, okay? I need you to open up a little, because there's stuff we need to–"

"Why won't you have sex with me?" she snapped suddenly, her head coming up to look me dead in the eyes.

I stopped breathing. "Uh, what?" I managed to sputter out.

Her green eyes narrowed. "You're so careful with me. *Too* careful. Do you..." she sighed and I could tell she was losing steam. "Do you not want to..."

I choked out a humourless laugh. "Anna, *please.* How could you even *think* that?"

"Because I'm not a mind reader either, okay?" she shouted, standing up and pacing around distractedly. "You just – you never make it clear."

I stood up, unable to take it any longer. She was faced away from me so I took her arm in my hand, pulling her around to look at me properly. "Anna, you have *no idea* how much I want to, okay? Every single fibre of me wants to, I *promise*. God, every time I look at you..."

She shook her head, looking into my eyes. "Then why don't you?"

I stuttered for a moment, the words stalling in my head. "Because we *shouldn't*."

Anna reeled back at this, confused. "We shouldn't? What the hell does that mean?"

I sighed and let go of her arm, immediately missing the feeling of her skin against mine.

"It shouldn't be me, Anna. Not to – to be with you like that. God, I want to *so* badly, I swear. But it shouldn't be like that between us, I – I'm not here for that."

Her face screwed up in rage and I knew that I'd said the wrong thing. "You're not? Well what the fuck are you here for, then? Unless there's something you *know* that I don't."

My still heart nearly jumped out of my chest. "*No!*" I shouted. "We just can't–"

"Why not?" she shouted, her eyes blazing.

"Because I'm not *real!*" I shouted back, the words were out before I could take them back.

Her face softened slightly. "What?"

I sighed, rubbing my palms over my face to try and relieve some tension.

"Finding out who I am – who I *was*, I mean? It changed *nothing*, Anna. I'm still *here*, with only you to see me. I'm still silent to *everyone* except you. And spending time with you, God, it's been better than *any* life I could have had when I was alive."

Anna's eyes filled with emotion. "I know. But then, why–"

"Because I'm *dead*, Anna." I answered bluntly, shrugging. "I'm not real and I can't be with you like that because you deserve better, okay?"

"Why should *you* be the judge of what I deserve?!" Anna snapped. "I'm an adult, okay? I can decide for myself what's good for me."

"Clearly you can't. Because if you could, you wouldn't choose me." I said simply.

She scoffed, outraged and took a couple of steps back from me, shaking her head. Hurt showed clearly on her face and my chest ached for having caused it, but I stood firm where I was, resisting the urge to go over and pull her close to me.

"This is bullshit," she said quietly, "this is all about *you*. *You're* the one who feels like you're not enough, because you don't know who you are. But you don't need to feel like that! I like everything about who you are *now*, it doesn't *matter* to me that you've lost that part of you. It *never* mattered to me, okay? You're holding back from me because of *you*, not me."

"You're crazy." I snapped back at her, losing my patience with the chords striking painfully in my chest.

She threw her hands up in the air in frustration. "This *is* crazy! Everything about this situation is crazy, okay? I *wish* you would just be crazy with me and let go of all this shit that you're holding onto! Because whether you think so or not, you give me *everything* that I need and *more* than I could ever deserve, okay? You're just being fucking stupid."

Rage started to pool in my stomach as she shook her head, muttering to herself.

"Thinking you know best... you're just in denial. If you were just *honest* with yourself–"

Something in me snapped before I could even register that it was frayed. Before I even knew what I was doing, I was shouting with everything that I had.

"You want me to be *honest?* Fine!" She was taken aback at my tone, staring at me with the most infuriatingly beautiful eyes. "Being dead *hurts*, okay? It *hurts* me! I hate it! I want to feel the fucking sun on my face! I want to be able to *talk* to strangers, I want to be able to pet fucking dogs on the street! But I can't! And it kills me to see *you* hurting! About Charlie, about your family and all of it! But neither of those are even the worst hurt I feel, okay?! Because the *worst* hurt I feel, the worst hurt I could probably *ever* feel, is the one I feel every time I look at you!"

Anna frowned, hurt and confused. "What do you mean?"

I laughed with no humour, unable to believe that she didn't know what I was talking about.

"You really don't know?" I shouted, exasperated. "God, Anna! Can't you tell how much I want to give you *everything?*"

"But you *do...*" she started, but I knew she still didn't understand.

"No – I want to have *everything* with you, Anna! I want to actually *meet* your friends, instead of just standing in a room where they can't see me! I want to meet your parents! I want to come to your fucking graduation and not just stand in the background where only you can see me! I want to eat dinners with you and go on dates with you and – shit – I can't *believe* you don't know how much I want to have sex with you, because every time we touch I feel like all my cells are on fire and pulling me towards you– but... But I *can't*, okay? I can't give you those things, I can't give you everything and I'm not supposed to be that person to you. And, fuck, that *kills* me because I'm *so* in love with you and–"

"You– *what?*" Anna's eyes were enormous now and she was as still as a statue.

I hung my head for a moment, embarrassment flushing through me like a wave of boiling water. Well, that was *definitely* honest.

"Yes, Anna, *of course* I'm in love with you. God, how could I not be?"

She was walking towards me, taking careful, measured steps. I couldn't stop my words now, they flowed out of me like a creek that had just been unblocked, the water running clear and cold.

"Nothing could have stopped me from falling for you, I swear." I shrugged helplessly. "Not even all of this."

Anna was standing in front of me, almost expressionless, her green eyes wide and breath-taking.

"God, those eyes." I sighed, bringing one of my hands up to cup her face. "I want to be alive so badly, just to see these eyes every day."

"They're right here." Anna whispered, still looking at me in earnest.

I shook my head slowly. "Anna, no. It's not the same, it can never be real and you–"

"Please, just stop." she said quietly and I did. Carefully, she placed her hand on my chest and warmth flooded through my body, grounding me, tying me to her with a thousand invisible threads. "*This is real*, okay? You are here with me and I am here with you. And it's complicated and it's *crazy*, but it *is real*. I don't want anything else, or anyone else."

She was so close to me now, I could feel her heart beating through her chest and I wanted to press my lips to her neck so badly that it was making me ache.

"But God, I want you *so* badly." she whispered and I barely heard it for all the spinning in my head. My fingers grazed the skin of her waist and I couldn't stop them from moving beneath her t-shirt. Everything in my body was buzzing, like she was overwhelming my senses. When she spoke, I couldn't stop watching the way that her lips moved. "I've never wanted *anything* the way that I want you."

I sighed, my heart in my throat. I leaned into her until our bodies were almost pressed together and brought my lips down to her ear, placing a kiss on her neck just below it.

"Tell me you love me." I whispered in her ear, bringing my hands down to circle around her wrists.

When she looked at me her dark eyelashes cast a shadow on her cheeks and she breathed in deeply.

"I love y–"

I couldn't even let her finish before I grabbed her by the waist and crushed her to me. Every part of my half-alive body wanted her closer, touching me, pulling at me. My lips interlocked with hers over and over feverishly, desperately, her hands were at my back, clawing at it like she couldn't get hold of me properly.

All thoughts of anything else flew from my head when she pressed her lips to my neck and I couldn't take it anymore. Placing my hands back on her hips, I lifted her up and instinctively she wrapped her legs around my waist, never taking her lips from mine. I grabbed the back of her head with my hand, lacing my fingers into her hair and giving it a little tug as I kissed her. As carefully as I could, I walked us both over to the bed and placed her down there, laughing a little when she whined because I took my lips away from hers for a moment.

Slowly she crawled back to lean against the bedframe, her long hair falling in waves that grazed her sides. When she looked at me, unsmiling, that determined look in her jade eyes, I couldn't breathe properly. I leaned over and tried to kiss her gently, chastely, but couldn't help but groan in want when I felt her tongue sweep across mine.

"Please..." she whispered between heavy kisses, "please don't stop this time."

I almost laughed, shaking my head as I tugged her t-shirt up over her head.

"Never." I whispered back to her, leaving a trail of kisses across her chest, then slowly down her stomach.

Never. I could never stop. She was there with me, all warm porcelain skin and ardent eyes. Dark hair that curled down her bare back. Small moans that echoed in my mind like she was singing just for me. *She* was the angel. My angel.

CHAPTER 10

TOGETHER

THEY WERE ONE now. Before, it had felt like they were living different lives, overlapping occasionally, never *together*.

"We have to go." Anna announced to the dark of the room.

"Go? Go where?"

She shifted and looked towards Joe, laying next to her on the bed. The moonlight from the window refracted delicately through the edges of his head, his hair slightly untidy like glass fibres.

"To Montpellier, of course. We have to follow the clue on the postcard. It's our strongest lead." she considered for a moment, "Our only *lead*, really."

"But what if we went all that way and found nothing – it would be a complete waste of time. Besides, think of the cost."

"No. I've thought about that." She sat up in bed cross-legged and looked down at him. "I've got a little put away – for a holiday, or if the car gives up or something, so it wouldn't matter." She paused for a reaction, but he was quietly listening to her, "Besides, at this time of year flights and accommodation would be cheap enough before the rush for Christmas hits."

She sprang off the bed towards her desk, suddenly motivated and opened up her laptop. Her face glowed in the darkness from the screen; she looked back to the bed. Joe's eyes were sparkling in the light of the laptop. "Come on, let's see if we can find a flight."

Joe was supremely comfortable on the bed. Although he couldn't really feel it, he had convinced himself that he was warm and snug – so the grunts and complaints that he made heaving himself to his feet were more from the mental effort than anything physical.

"You sound like an old man." she joked as he joined her and leaned in to the screen.

Anna typed some details into a last-minute flights website and waited for the results to appear. Within a few seconds several results came up. "Oh, look that's not too bad. One hundred and fifty two pounds, return."

"You only selected one passenger." Joe spotted.

"Of course, silly." She nudged him with her elbow which sank partly into his side. He jumped back; thankfully he saw the humour in it. "Oh, yes." He realised why she'd done that, "I can hardly get a plane ticket if I'm dead."

"No passport either!" Anna said, rubbing his side as if she'd hurt him. "That would have been *very* useful."

"Okay, then. So, when do we go?" Joe asked.

Anna clicked a few times, closing in on an exact date. "The day after tomorrow, for three nights." she announced, "That should be enough, shouldn't it?"

"I guess so," Joe replied thoughtfully. "I wish I could remember what it was like there, I could suggest a good place to stay."

"Let's take a look at the area." Anna typed the address on the postcard into Google Maps. Straight away, the map appeared. She clicked on the button to show the satellite image. "Wow, that place must have cost an absolute bomb. Look, it's right next to the marina."

Joe whistled in admiration. Even *he* was impressed. "Do you think my folks own one of those yachts moored there?"

"That would be insane!" Anna replied, pulling Joe closer. She zoomed back in a little on the map. "Oohh, look, a big camping area just next to where your parents' house is. There's a pool too."

Joe leaned in further, pressing as best he could against Anna's shoulder. "So, that's the place then." he said with a faraway voice. "I guess, I must have spent my summers there, grown up there... Pan up a little on the map would you?"

The map scrolled down revealing a small theme park. It looked a little sad and dilapidated from above. There were photos posted by the public in the panel to the side; they painted a different picture – it looked like a really fun place to go. "Guess, I'd have spent a lot of time there too." he said wistfully. "Hung out with the other kids in the area."

"Perhaps there was a girl there too?" Anna suggested. They both sat in silence for a couple of moments. Neither of them had considered that he had a girlfriend while he was alive. "It's not impossible," Anna said, voice shaking a little, "a good looking guy like you, rich..."

Joe shook his head dismissively, "No. I don't think so. I'd have appeared to her then wouldn't I, not you." The seed of doubt had been planted in his head now but he wouldn't accept it.

Anna brightened, trying to change the subject

before they became morose. "Let's see if we can book a place at the camp site then." said Anna, clicking on a link on the map. "Oh, it's chalets. Looks okay." She clicked and typed for a couple of minutes, muttering occasionally as she checked dates and availability. Joe had drifted off to the window and was looking outside. It was perfectly still, cold – well, he assumed it was cold out.

Breaking out of his reverie, he turned and put his hands gently on Anna's shoulders. "How are you getting on?"

"Not too bad," she started, "Lots of availability this time of year. I'm going to go ahead and book the flight and the chalet." She leaned her head back to look up at Joe above her. "Exciting! We're going off on holiday." She grinned cheesily, up at him.

"Cute." he replied quietly, kissing her on the forehead. "Like a proper couple." But there was still a hint of sadness in his voice.

Early December sunlight streamed through the vast expanse of glass winking periodically behind the mighty metal framework. Anna was used to the rather crowded check-in halls at the other terminal, but the giant envelope of glass that surrounded Terminal 5 at London Heathrow airport seemed almost empty by comparison.

The wheels on Anna's hand luggage hummed quietly across the polished floor as they made their way to the check-in desk.

Joe had been quiet the whole coach journey and was still somewhat subdued. The coach was mostly empty and they'd sat far towards the back, away from the handful of other passengers so that they could talk. But they had only exchanged a handful of words.

She knew that Joe was nervous about what they might find at their destination, so she made a point of not pressing him. Perhaps there was more to it?

"You're not nervous about flying are you?" she said quietly; he was walking in lockstep alongside her.

"No. Well, I don't think so." he muttered, "At least–" but the rest of what he said was drowned out by an announcement over the PA.

"Sorry, I didn't catch that." She looked over to him, the light in here wasn't kind to him – he seemed to be blending in to the glass of the building.

"Don't worry about it, I was just gabbling." he replied.

They reached the check-in desk. There was only a short queue and in just a few minutes they were into the security area. There were a lot more people in here filtering through from the endless row of check-in desks outside. But the queue moved quickly and before long, she was stepping nervously through the scanner, praying that it didn't go off.

She glanced behind her as she crossed over to the conveyor to collect her bag. Joe was still standing at the *wait* line. What was he doing? He suddenly twigged and quickly darted through just ahead of an Asian-looking lady, sliding past her as she passed under the scanner.

The scanner beeped and the lady began patting her pockets, embarrassed, for any stray keys or coins.

"Was that you?" Anna muttered under her breath.

"I don't know, maybe. Those things are pretty

sensitive – perhaps the Ghostbusters could do with one of those!" Anna couldn't help letting a laugh escape. A severe looking customs woman glared at her from the other side of the belt.

That had done it, the mood was broken. Joe seemed more his usual self as they stepped out into the main concourse filled with shops, bars, places to eat.

"I've got an idea." she said and accelerated off in the direction of the shops.

Next to the little store selling obnoxious souvenirs of London was a large electronics store.

"Wait here." she ordered, "Just in case you set off the alarms again." She gestured discretely to the security tag detectors. Joe grinned and stepped back.

A couple of minutes later, Anna emerged from the shop with a plastic blister pack. She took a seat in the central seating area and with a bit of effort opened it and held it in her lap for Joe to see.

"I don't get it." he said. "What do you need one of those for?"

Anna clipped the Bluetooth microphone onto her ear and made a show of fiddling with her phone. "Joe. Hi," she began in a slightly exaggerated voice, "I'm at the airport... Yes, all good. I got a little headset for my phone so that I can talk with you more easily." There was nobody behind Joe, so she winked at him.

Joe doubled up laughing. Boy, she was smart.

"Look, we've got about an hour before the gate opens. Let's go get a coffee." Although she was looking directly at Joe, standing right in front of her, to everyone else she was just looking into space talking on the phone.

Deftly, Anna shimmied into the vacant seat at a little round table the instant a weary-looking businessman got up to leave. It was the only place left in the coffee shop. A woman standing nearby in an expensive-looking suit rolled her eyes at her. Anna gestured to the other seat opposite her on the little metal table but the woman scoffed and tapped her foot impatiently.

Sure now that the woman wasn't going to take up the seat, Joe slid into the empty space. He didn't need to sit, his legs didn't tire, but he wanted to sit and look at Anna.

She pretended to press the button on her headset "You know what's making me the most nervous?" she asked.

"Breaking the news to my parents?" Joe replied. He knew that this would be particularly awkward – a hundred times more so than turning up on Leo's doorstep.

"Yes." she said, picking a blueberry out of her extortionately expensive muffin. "I've absolutely no idea what to say. In fact, I'm pretty sure that I don't want to talk with them if we don't find anything – is that okay?"

"No, that's fine." He laid his hand on the table and let her put hers in his. "I reckon that you might not need to approach them to begin with. If we find something, then we... you, could just take it to the police and let *them* do the dirty work."

Anna let out a long sigh of relief. "You're right. I might not need to get involved at all. I don't think that I could handle more grief. Especially if... what on earth?" Anna trailed off, distracted by the impatient woman from earlier who was now berating a woman with a toddler and a baby. The mother was struggling to feed the baby from a bottle, while the toddler cheerfully destroyed a bun of sorts.

"What's *her* problem?" Anna said into her hand. Joe leaned over to get a better listening position.

"What a cow!" he said after a minute. "She's asking her to leave because she's only bought a bun and no drink. Thinks she gets to sit there because her friend is coming soon with coffees."

The young mother looked up, flustered, gathered her things and started to leave. Joe's jaw actually dropped when the woman took a seat at the table, then snapped her fingers at a member of staff who was busy filling the paper napkin dispenser. When the old man gestured that he would be over in a minute, she huffed and swept the bits of broken bun and other trash onto the floor.

"What an entitled bitch!" Joe fumed, "I'd bloody slap her if I could!"

Anna waved at the woman with the children as she struggled with her suitcase. She looked over, close to tears.

"Here, take my table. I'm leaving." she shouted over, making sure that the nasty woman could hear. She pretended not to, busying herself with rummaging about in her designer handbag.

"That was a cool move." Joe said to Anna as they approached a display board. "That kind of person just makes me lose my mind."

"Do you think you're remembering bits of your past

life?" Anna mused. She looked up at the board to find their flight.

"I don't know. I still can't remember anything that happened in my life apart from that one flashback. I suppose my *character* is all that has remained intact."

"Hmmm. Ah, look, that's our gate." She started to point, then remembered herself just in time and scratched the side of her head. Joe chuckled.

They didn't have to wait very long at the gate and there were enough seats, even for Joe – though he had stay alert, lest someone came along and sat on him.

A member of the airline staff appeared at the desk and invited the priority passengers to begin boarding. Most of the rest of the passengers started to gather their things and an orderly queue began to form, ready for the remainder of the boarding.

Anna remained seated. There was no rush and besides it would be easier for Joe if they got onto the plane near the end.

Just then, a face they both recognised. A couple of people including an old lady with a stick were still in the short, priority queue getting their boarding passes checked. The rude lady from the coffee shop pushed to the front of the queue and slapped her passport down on the desk without a word. The woman checking tickets started to protest, pointing at the old lady with the stick. The old lady waved her hand dismissively and let it pass.

Joe grinned craftily at Anna. "Hang on, watch this." He sprinted off towards the boarding desk. They had installed new biometric scanners at the gate to make things faster and safer. Joe ducked through the scanner just as 'Karen' sauntered through." The gate beeped and the airline staff pulled her to one side. A ripple of sniggers went through the queue of passengers waiting to board. Anna had now joined the queue and watched the woman taking off her huge earrings.

She stepped back through the scanner and once more Joe darted through flipping a middle finger. The alarm went off and the woman had to subject herself to a frisk and check with a hand scanner. Off came the shoes this time.

Joe didn't relent and was rewarded with a frustrated scream from the woman as she threw her jacket into the plastic tray with her other belongings. The other passengers seemed mostly content to delay boarding for a few minutes in exchange for the free show. A couple were even filming the incident on their phones.

Feeling that justice had been served, Joe let the woman endure a fourth and final cycle before letting her through. A couple of passengers actually groaned when the scanner failed to go off. The woman grabbed her things and marched off down the tunnel to the plane barefoot and cursing.

Joe swaggered up to Anna and stood with her in the queue, quietly grinning. When it was her time to pass through, Joe carefully walked around it.

"You're awful." Anna hissed under her breath as they made their way down the connecting tunnel to the plane. "Hilarious, but awful."

Cleverly, Anna had taken advantage of the ability to choose her seat position from those remaining on the flight when she booked.

They picked their way slowly to the very back of the plane, stopping occasionally to let those in front heft luggage into the overhead compartment and organise themselves.

"I'm never going to get used to this." he grumbled as a woman swung a bag up and through his head.

Finally, they got to the back and he ducked past the toilets and loitered in the space next to the emergency doors. "I'm going to hang out back here until it's time to take off." he called.

Anna pressed a couple of fingers to the side of her head where she still had her headset. "Okay darling... yes, I'll see you later – love you. Bye." She smirked to herself getting to her feet to let a smartly dressed elderly man take his seat next to her.

She glanced back towards the exit where Joe was standing. He waved feebly at her.

Eventually, the cabin staff managed to get everyone settled and buckled in. As the plane began to taxi towards the runway they ran through the safety presentation. Anna rolled her eyes when she looked about to see almost nobody watching. She always felt sorry for the cabin crew at this point in the flight.

She jumped when she felt a soft pressure on her shoulder. Joe had come out of hiding and was standing in the aisle next to her. The plane trundled on for a couple more minutes, then she felt it gently turn ninety degrees and without ceremony, the pilot throttled up and they were thundering down the runway. The plane clattered and shook as it gained speed but for some reason Joe remained standing as if they were completely motionless, his touch on her shoulder steady and light as a feather. Suddenly there was a thump and they were airborne and still accelerating, the nose of the plane lifting up high, pushing Anna back into her seat.

She glanced to her left to see Joe calmly standing in place, but with the angle of the plane it appeared as if he was leaning back at a crazy angle. Eventually, they levelled out and as the air thinned, the engine noise subsided to a more comfortable background whine.

A couple of minutes later, the familiar ping of the seatbelt sign sounded. The instant the light went out most passengers felt the need to unbuckle. Anna left hers on as usual and relaxed back into her seat. She placed her hand onto her shoulder where Joe's had remained throughout ascent. Had he sensed that she was a little nervous about take-offs and landings?

"Ugh. Gotta go, back in a minute." He grumbled as a procession of passengers made their way towards the toilet at the back.

"Couldn't they have gone before we left?" she muttered to Joe as he backed up.

"Hmmm?" The gentleman next to her pulled an earbud out.

"Oh, sorry. I was talking to myself." she lied. The man went back to listening to his music.

Towards the front of the plane, where the curtain was drawn between them and business class, the staff were bringing out a trolley. Were drinks included? She wasn't sure. Joe was more or less trapped on the other side of two people waiting for the toilet so she decided to take a short walk to ask.

She had got about as far as the seats over the wing

when she heard a blood-curdling scream.

"Anna!!! Come back!" She whipped around to see why Joe was calling but where was he? Heart racing, she started walking quickly back. A man started to get up out of his seat ahead of her. "Anna! I'm sinking! Quickly!" Her blood turned to ice as she realised what was happening. Joe was only solid when he was near to her, and she had moved. *Oh God, he was going to fall through the plane!*

At the rear, Joe had suddenly felt the blast of wind throwing him backwards to the wall behind. His hair and ethereal clothes whipped and flapped, rushing filled his ears and he felt himself beginning to sink through the thin metal and plastic behind him.

She broke into a run, pushing the man backwards. He fell back, shouting. In seconds, she reached he toilet queue, but Joe was nowhere to be seen. She ducked her head to either side of the standing pair desperately trying to find him. She was about to barge through when a movement caught her eye, a glisten in the bulkhead ahead of her. Joe struggled and pushed his way through the wall from the compartment behind terrified and panting.

Anna gasped and bent double with relief.

"What's your problem?" The guy at the back of the queue sneered at her.

She was still in shock, but managed, "Dodgy tummy, and pointed to the locked door ahead."

"Sorry, lady. You gotta wait." the guy spat.

Anna waved it off and gestured that she could wait. The woman at the head of the queue had more sympathy though. The violent rush of the toilet flush burst through the thin door and a teenage girl emerged. The woman looked at Anna, "You go ahead love," and waved her though. Anna thanked the lady and sidled past the man, who muttered something under his breath.

Joe ducked into the toilet through the folding door just before it closed.

The instant that the lock slid into place, they threw themselves together. Anna sobbed quietly into Joe's shoulders, pulled back and smoothed his hair.

"Fuck, fuck, fuck, I thought I'd lost you!" she hissed, knowing that there were people just behind the thin door.

Joe was shaking still, and was it even possible that he looked pale? "I was vanishing, the *plane* was vanishing! Oh, God I thought I was going to fall out." This close, he was solid enough that she could feel him shivering.

"Stay close to me Joe, don't leave my side for the rest of the flight." She held him tightly, fingers grasping the short hair at the back of his head, pulling him tighter towards her.

"Don't worry," he breathed, "I'm not going to leave your side." The light in the cramped bathroom was dim, even so Joe seemed almost translucent now rather than glassy. The patterned wall behind was blurred through his body and he felt more solid than she had ever felt him.

Anna looked into his eyes, could she detect a hint of blue? She felt her lips brush against his. Without thinking, she pressed against him and let the moment flow over her in hot waves. His mouth was on her neck now as her head thrust back in silent ecstasy, his hands pushing into the small of her back, pressing her body into his. She felt him against her, pressing against her, his urgency almost corporeal now. His hands slid down to her buttocks, pulling her tighter towards him. The ache inside was building to an unbearable level, bordering on exquisite pain that threatened to engulf her. A soft moan escaped her parted lips as she imagined his hot breath on her face– a sharp rap on the door.

"Are you okay in there, my lovely?" It was the woman in the queue outside. The world came crashing back like a blast of cold water, the engine sounds returned to forgotten senses.

Joe backed away, a cheeky grin plastered over his face. Anna smirked, barely suppressing a laugh. They hadn't planned this at all.

"Er... Thanks, yes, I'm okay." she called through the door, then through her teeth to Joe. "Shit. I need to pee now. Turn around."

He dutifully did so while she relieved herself, freshened up and flushed. Instinctively, he held on to the edge of the sink at the sound of the sudden rush of air.

She motioned for him to move to the side, unlocked the door and folded it open. Anna grinned sheepishly at the woman outside who peered over her shoulder apprehensively after hearing the moans and groans coming through the door. Joe ducked behind her and took up position next to Anna's seat.

The drinks trolley had just about reached the back of the plane when Anna flopped down into her seat and fumbled about for the belt. When it arrived, she had made up her mind that she needed something a little stronger than an overpriced coffee and ordered an equally extortionate can of gin and tonic.

Deliciously warm air greeted Anna as she stepped outside at Montpellier Méditerranée Airport. The difference between the crisp winter air of Heathrow and the perfect Mediterranean climate was amazing.

"I see why your folks wanted to stay here." she said.

"Looks warm." Joe said, "Certainly a lot less gloomy. I was a lucky chap."

There were a row of smart, modern looking taxis a short way ahead with just a few people waiting in line. They joined the queue and Anna pulled out a page of notes from her pocket. She tipped the page towards Joe and nodded – the address of the camping park nearby.

When it was their turn, Anna held the door for a moment for Joe to slip inside then jumped in herself. She greeted the driver and gave him the address in perfect French. Joe raised his eyebrows, impressed.

"From England, yes?" The driver asked in English, pulling smoothly away.

"Ah," she chuckled, "you can tell?"

He was a huge man, with a laugh to match, "Oui, yes. A game I play to myself. But you speak French very well. Do you come here for your holidays by yourself, alone or others?" he asked.

"Oh, I'm staying here for a few days with my boyfriend." she said, smiling over to Joe sat proudly next to her.

"Ah. Bon. He is here now, or does he join you later?"

"No, he's here." Anna said with a grin, squeezing Joe's hand out of sight of the driver.

The sun was low over the sea as they sped along the costal roads towards Port Camargue. They pulled away from the coast and headed inland. Anna knew they were nearly there but wished that they could have driven longer. The warm evening sun on her cheek cheered her and glittered beautifully through Joe who also gazed longingly outside.

At the camping park, Anna handed the driver some Euros and thanked him in French while Joe hopped out through the open cab door.

The lady at reception took great pride in talking Anna through the facilities on offer at the park and went to great effort to extol the virtues of the restaurant and café bar. The water park was closed this time of year, but the pools were open to residents.

The receptionist handed Anna a map of the site with her keys onto which she circled their cabin in red biro.

"You take your holiday alone?" The receptionist asked, finally in English.

Anna decided on a more plausible story since she would be snooping around for a couple of days. "Oh, no I'm here writing a news story for my paper back in England." She glanced sideways at Joe for an instant and continued in French, "About the boy that died here recently. Have you heard about that?"

The woman's face grew sombre. "Yes, I know who you're talking about. I didn't know him personally but he used to hang about at the amusement park with some local kids. Nice enough boy, I hear but... well, trouble with his parents."

"Trouble?" Anna asked. Some new information so soon?

"Well, you know, the usual teenager sort of thing. Rebellious, I think. Anyway, that's about all anyone knows. He disappeared one day, never came back."

Their cabin, when they found it in the maze of almost identical looking static homes seemed in good condition. Inside, seemed clean. A faint aroma of cigarette smoke lingered but not so bad it couldn't be ignored.

"I didn't know you spoke French," Joe's voice floated from the front of the cabin, a cosy living room. Anna had checked out the kitchen then headed straight for the bedroom and flung herself onto the bed with a contented sigh.

She giggled. "There's a lot you don't know about me. Got a grade 9 in GCSE French – top score in the whole year." she announced proudly. "Had a French pen-pal for a few years too."

Joe felt a little pang of jealousy, "You had a French boyfriend?" He was standing at the doorway now.

"No, silly." She lifted her head up to smile at him, "Her name was Michelle. Lived in Nantes – happy?" she jibed. "Come on," She patted the bed, "I think I need a nap before we do anything."

"Sure," Joe began as he slid onto the bed. He brushed a strand of hair from her face. "But don't you think we should finish what we started in the mile-high club?"

CHAPTER 11

JOE

IT'S THE NIGHT time that I really dread. That's the time that I'm alone, truly alone because there's literally nobody on the planet that I can talk with when she's asleep. All I can do is drift about – not in the cartoon ghost kind of way, I just pace or stand at the window and look outside. I guess the scenes in movies where the camera pans to the upstairs window of a house and there's a face there makes sense to me now. All we ghosts have to do is mope about unless we have someone special that can hear us.

There's a little porch outside with some tatty plastic garden furniture on it. I decide to spend a while out there, listening to the night sounds. The door is thin and flimsy and although I can't quite manage the handle, I can push through the plastic with a bit of effort – like a 'proper' ghost.

Even at this hour there's a constant sound of cars on the nearby main road, occasionally there's a motorbike tearing up the road. Somewhere far off, maybe by the beach there's some music playing, a random shout from kids enjoying the night.

A couple walked past our cabin on the way to theirs, slightly unsteadily. "Evening." I called out cheerfully, but of course they just wandered by.

Eventually, even the kids on the beach called it a night and the music shut off. I listened carefully to the sudden stillness, a break in the traffic. Then a couple of mopeds razzed and sped off.

I watched the stars move slowly over the back shapes of the mountains and across the cloudless, sky. Even the moon had shunned me this evening.

In time, the stars dragged a milky light over the mountains and I knew that dawn would come soon. I headed back inside and lay on the bed, watching and waiting for Anna to wake.

TOGETHER

The lady from yesterday brought Anna pain-au-chocolate and coffee at the poolside café bar. She learned that her name was Annette and they laughed a little about how similar their names were.

"Do you have plans for today?" she asked. Her English was good, but Anna guessed that so was her German and Spanish in this line of business.

"Yeah. More research for my story." She took a gulp of the strong, black coffee. "Do they keep the records of deaths here in Port Camargue?"

"Oh, no not anymore; they used to years ago, but the records office has closed down. You need to go into Montpellier for that. The library has public records for the whole region." She smiled at a couple who had taken a seat nearby. "The bus stops just outside the camp entrance."

Anna thanked her as she left to attend to the new customers. "That's handy." She said under her breath to Joe then rummaged in her bag for the headset. "Don't want anyone to think I'm crazy."

For some reason, Anna had images of rifling through

dusty records in a basement office. She pulled her chair closer to the screen in the little booth and typed in the access code that the librarian had given her.

The main menu appeared and she quickly found the deaths register. The search form was simple enough – one area to type the name, more fields to type in to narrow the results.

The cursor blinked patiently, ominously. Joe laid his hand on Anna's shoulder, "It's okay, let's do it."

She typed, 'Joe Brooks'. Even though Joe couldn't read French at the moment, he could tell that the screen showed 'No Results.' She tried again, 'Joseph Brooks'... nothing. She thought for a moment, then tried 'Joey Brooks'.

"Okay, how about..." she typed just 'Brooks'. Three entries, Madeline Brooks in 1978, Claude Brooks in 1982 and Jacques Brooks in 2004. She sighed. "Well, I guess it was a long shot." she said. Joe's hand was still on her shoulder, she put hers on top of his.

"The papers then?" he said.

There was a section where the local papers had been digitised and could be searched. She entered the keywords in French, 'boy; missing; Port Camargue'.

The results came back so quickly that it caught Anna by surprise. Part of her wasn't expecting to find anything so specific. She clicked on the link and let out a shuddering gasp. Joe recoiled from the screen. There, at the head of a short article was a black and white photograph of Joe, taken presumably with some friends though they had been mostly cropped out, just their shoulders showing to either side. He was grinning into the camera, sitting atop a dirt-bike.

"This is it, isn't it?" rasped Joe from behind. Anna nodded silently and started reading.

"... English boy, Joe Brooks, missing June..." She trailed off. Choking. "June 5th. That's the day Charlie had his accident."

Joe tensed, gripping Anna's shoulder. "Oh, crap. That explains a lot doesn't it? That's the connection."

Anna was trembling slightly, she read on softly, her voice quavering. "... left parents' holiday home on motorcycle after an argument... whereabouts unknown... no body found, or sightings after over a week." Anna stopped reading and sat in grim silence.

"So that's it. We both died in a motorcycle accident. But they found your brother."

Anna nodded. Her eyes were brimming with tears, "Yes. At the bottom of a cliff. He was out at night while we were on holiday in Cornwall." It was tearing her apart to talk about it, but the time was right to talk now. "I *told* him it was a stupid idea." She sniffed, "But he wouldn't listen." She turned to him, "You did the same. You rode out that night, angry and killed yourself."

He hung his head, "I must have." He looked into Anna's eyes, streaming with tears, "What did I do? Where did I go?"

"The postcard." Anna remembered, fumbling in her bag for her phone. "Something you said about going away on a boat?" She started searching for the photo she took at Leo's house.

"Yes, that's right. Did I go to the Marina, looking for a friend's boat?"

Anna read from the photo of the postcard, *"Jean Luc*

says that we should just take off for a week on his Dad's boat if it gets too much. Remember the one? You got so drunk when you came over that one time, you ended up trying to climb up on the bull by the carousel"

"If I went off on a boat, maybe fell overboard then there's *no* way we'd be able to find me."

"I don't think that's what happened. It's got to be the motorbike thing, it wouldn't make sense otherwise." Anna said.

"But the marina's only a short distance from my parents' house. If I'd had an accident on the way there it would have been obvious."

"The carousel though, it has to be close. There's that amusement park nearby." Anna scratched her head.

"We should head back, there's bound to be a clue around the amusement park." Joe suggested.

Anna agreed. They were certainly on the right track and the papers and records wouldn't be able to help otherwise there would be a follow-up story. The paper was a dead end now.

The bus pulled away from the layby in front of the camping park leaving Anna squinting across the dusty road towards the amusement park. Even for the time of the year, the mid afternoon sun was making her long for the air-conditioned bus she had just left.

There was only the sound of insects now as they approached the empty car park. They walked across the empty parking spaces to the main gate and ticket office.

The entrance was closed, the gate in front chained up for the off-season. Anna peered through. There was a large map of the park showing the location of all the rides. She looked quizzically at Joe.

"No carousel?" he said, guessing her thoughts.

"No carousel." she echoed back. "I don't see any bull either, do you?"

"If it's one of those rodeo things, it'll be inside, I guess. It won't be on the map."

"Can I help you?" A man emerged from round the side of the ticket office and spoke to them in French, making Anna start. He looked at them through the gate, eyeing them suspiciously.

"Oh, sorry. I didn't see you there." she replied, "We're doing a scavenger hunt with our tour group."

The man took the scruffy cigarette out of his mouth, picked a stray strand of tobacco from his lip and flicked it away. He peered past Anna, looking round the cracked wall. "We?"

"Um, yes, the rest of the group is... somewhere about." Her heart was racing, Joe looked at her nervously.

"It's okay, we're not doing anything wrong. Keep going." he urged.

"Yeah, er, we need to find a carousel with a bull nearby not far from the marina."

The man began laughing wheezily. "*Mademoiselle*, you're in completely the wrong place. Kilometres away."

Anna flushed, but this was something – he seemed to know the place they were looking for. Joe still had no idea what was going on and was looking angrily at the man who appeared to be making fun of Anna.

"The wrong place?" she began, calmly, "Where do we need to be?"

He took a puff of his roll-up and pointed with it somewhere south. "Saintes Maries-de-la-mer." He laughed again, "The marina there. There's an antique carousel on the promenade, and next to it a sculpture." He looked Anna in the eye, "That's the bull you're searching for." With that, he wandered off chuckling and muttering to himself.

Anna stepped to the side of the gate behind the wall where she could be sure that the man couldn't see her, though at this point she really didn't care.

"That's the place!" she said, beaming, "The place you were heading for. There's another marina along the coast. That must have been where your friend's parents' boat is." She threw her arms around Joe and held him tightly.

"Makes sense," he said, "If I was going to get away from my parents I'd have gone further than the marina here. So, where's this place?"

Anna broke away and began tapping on her phone. She zoomed in on the place that the man had mentioned. "Yes! That's it, look!" Sure enough, the satellite photo showed a small harbour with boats moored in it and right next to it, the circular shape of the carousel.

Joe took a step back, hands clasped behind his head. He paced a little. This was it, they were so close to finding out where and maybe how he had died. Anna had gone quiet. She was slowly swiping at her phone, face ashen.

"What's up?" said Joe, concerned now.

"There's something else." she said flatly. Despite the sun, she felt a chill run right through her. "Another connection."

"How so?" Joe stepped closer to see what was on her phone. She had been checking the route from here. The images from the map's street view said it all. "Oh, crap." he said. Anna tapped on the screen a couple of times and the image jumped forwards along the road – the coastal road – winding along several miles of cliff face dropping down to the sea below.

"Well," he said shakily, "we know how I died then."

"Just like poor Charlie" Anna said, sadly. "Except that clearly, they never found you."

"You think I'm still at the bottom of a cliff somewhere?"

"It all points to that, yes. It adds up – that's why you can't cross over, or whatever it is. That must be the last piece of the puzzle. We have to find your body."

"Oh, man." He shook his head, "That's grim. So what do we do? There's miles of road between here and that other place... Saint, something?"

"Saintes Maries-de-la-mer," she corrected, "I think we need to travel the road, see if you can pick up anything. Honestly, I don't know what else there is to do. We can't just go to the police and ask them to search again, they won't listen to me."

"It's a long way to walk..." but then it dawned on him, "Oh. I see. We have to go by moped don't we?"

"I think that's probably how it works; the universe seems to be cruel like that." She shoved her phone back into her bag, "Come on then, let's see if we can get ourselves some wheels. I saw a notice in the camp reception about moped hire, but I didn't give it much thought."

"No. Sorry, they're closed now." Annette said sadly. *Did she ever have a break?* Anna wondered. She always seemed to be there, or at the café. "They open between ten am and noon this time of year."

"Where do I go to hire?" Anna asked. She was a little frustrated about having to wait until tomorrow, but she didn't let it show.

"Just over the other side of the camp." She pointed to the larger map on the wall behind the reception desk. "I'll let them know you want to hire. I'll tell them to give you a clean one." she laughed. *I don't mind if it's clean or not, so long as the brakes are good.* Anna thought to herself.

They walked back to their cabin; Anna was clutching a cold bottle of Orangina which she bought at reception. She'd not had that for years, though she was a little disappointed that it was in a plastic bottle rather than the cute light-bulb shaped glass one she remembered.

"You do realise that tomorrow might be our last day together if you cross over?" she said sadly.

"I do." Joe replied. "It's tearing me apart. I know I can't stay here – that the *reason* I appeared to you was that you'd be able to help me find peace." They stepped up onto the wooden deck of the porch and Anna pulled the bulky key ring out of her bag. Hot air boiled out from the poorly insulated static home and made Anna gasp.

She put her bottle down on the table in the family room and moved close to Joe. "It kills me too. Finally, I find someone that *gets me*, that puts up with all my shit only to lose you." She laid her head on his shoulder, enjoying the silky softness of his form against hers. "The worst thing is that I'm cheerfully helping that happen. What's wrong with me, I–"

"There's *nothing* wrong with you," Joe silenced her before she could beat herself up any more. "You're the kindest, most thoughtful person. You've had some bad breaks, and sure that's messed you up a little. But you're tough... when I'm gone–" Anna started to say something, but he put his finger softly to her lips, "When I'm gone, you'll know that you did the right thing."

"But I don't want you to go." Her voice was anguish, but she knew he *had* to.

"It can't work. I'll never age. I'll still be like this when you're ninety, young... *fit*, my appearance mocking you. Then one day you'll be gone and we'll *never* be together again."

"What do you mean never?"

"I'll be trapped. If only you can help me pass on, if you die then I can't, ever."

"Shit." She thought for a moment. "So... does that mean that, you know, *eventually*, I'll see you again?"

He pulled her tightly to him, "I don't know, I honestly don't."

"I don't think I ever *really* believed in the afterlife and all that." She sniffed, "Shit, I didn't even believe in ghosts really before you came along. But this changes everything. Perhaps I might see you... after, then."

"Perhaps. I think that should be something that you could hang on to, but please – live your life. Don't save yourself for me. If you find love, grab it. Remember me but don't let me haunt you after I'm gone."

Anna sighed. She knew he was right.

"Let's make our last night a little special." Joe began. "We're in the South of France, our work is nearly done. Let's enjoy it. Grab dinner by the sea, watch the sun go down, walk on the beach – all that kind of thing."

"You're just guessing that's what a girl wants, aren't you?" she said, smiling a little.

"Busted." he admitted.

"Sounds good though. I'm in. But I'm knackered. You mind if I take a shower and a little nap first? I'm not made for this heat."

"Lightweight, it's nearly winter!" he joked. Anna punched him on the arm, but it was like hitting a pillow.

The bathroom was tiny, the shower cubical was plasticky and creaky when she moved about in there, and the water wasn't very hot... or powerful for that matter. But it felt good to cool down a little.

She didn't dare tell him the thought that flashed through her mind a couple of minutes ago. That she should kill herself after he crossed over, so they could be together. But she knew that was wrong. *Suicides go straight to hell*, she recalled from somewhere. That can't *always* be right, she thought – some people were just at the end of their tether, they weren't *bad*. No, it's not the way. She felt a little guilty now; her troubles seemed so petty by comparison with anyone that felt that the only way forward was to end their own life.

CHAPTER 12

THERE WERE ABOUT twenty shabby looking mopeds lined up on the path outside the hire office. During the summer, they would have done a roaring trade renting these out to holidaymakers. They terrified Anna. She'd seen this kind of outfit plenty of times before, renting out poorly maintained machines to just about anyone, no questions asked.

She was a little surprised when the young lad that seemed to be in charge asked for her passport and details for insurance. Insurance? That was new! Maybe it was just another way of extracting twenty more euros from the punters.

The boy gave her passport back after he'd photocopied it and made her sign a badly copied form. She didn't read it, most likely it was either just nonsense or a bunch of disclaimers indemnifying the owners against death, damage and litigation.

"You know how to work it, yes?" the boy asked.

"Um, yeah." she replied uncertainly. She *did* know how to ride, but right now she was holding on to the machine that had killed the two loves in her life. She looked at the boy suddenly remembering. "Crash helmet?"

He looked back at her, blank-eyed. She'd used the right word hadn't she? "Crash helmet." she repeated in English, miming putting it on.

"Uh, okay." He reluctantly walked into the large wooden storage shed they seemed to be using as a workshop and lock-up. There were some mutterings, he called to someone in there who seemed to be 'fixing' something by hitting it. The hammering stopped for a few seconds and the boy emerged triumphantly holding an elderly looking cycle helmet. It was better than nothing – barely, so she accepted it and put it on. It fit well, surprisingly.

"Back by four. Okay?" he said in English. Hardly a full day's rental but they wouldn't need it for longer than that, hopefully.

With the headset connected to her phone, Anna started the navigation route that she had planned over breakfast. The calm voice in her ear announced the direction she should take.

The little engine started easily enough with a small puff of bluish smoke out the back which cleared quickly. Joe climbed on behind and put his arms around Anna.

"Okay. Let's do it." he breathed nervously in her free ear.

The boy looked on, slightly puzzled. What was she waiting for?

Slowly, Anna eased the moped forwards, the little engine razzing crudely. The road here was the main one that lead back into town but there was little flowing in the direction they were heading.

Joe could feel the tension in Anna's body as they drove along the road. He peered over her shoulder and saw tight white knuckles gripping the handlebars.

"Relax. You're doing just fine." he said. Somehow, his voice carried over the wind and she heard him as clearly as if he were the sat nav voice.

"I'm shitting myself," she laughed nervously. "and we haven't even got to the coast road yet."

"You'll be okay." He gave her a little squeeze and she giggled. Joe knew that this must be terrifying for her. He could only imagine the thoughts that must have been going around in her head about her poor brother and his accident. Was she also thinking about him? But they would be okay. Both accidents happened at night. The sky was bright and clear this morning, no wind, dry roads and the traffic was almost non-existent now that they had passed the marina.

He decided not to distract her just yet with further 'reassurance' – let her concentrate on the driving.

The sea glittered invitingly to their right, cool and blue in the morning sun. People were already starting to arrive at the beach, some walking their dogs, a group of boys up ahead making their way hopefully towards the sea with their sailboards. Not much wind, he thought. They'd do better at the quiet beach further south where the land jutted out into the sea– Wait. How had he known that?

"Something new!" he shouted. The bike swerved slightly, "Sorry, sorry!" he yelled.

"There's no need to shout." Anna called, her own advice unheeded. "I can still hear you in my head." She thought for a moment, "Can't say I'd noticed that until now – what was it?"

"I think I'm remembering things. I think I used to go surfing or sailboarding near here."

"Brilliant!" she called over the tinny buzz of the engine. "That must mean we're getting close."

The road was beginning to climb very slightly as

they neared the end of the breath-taking long stretch of beach. Up ahead, they could see the cliffs looming. Anna shivered and pushed the little moped a little harder.

They continued along the road for another ten or fifteen minutes in silence. The road had narrowed and the traffic all but evaporated, turning off onto the inland roads or favouring the newer larger routes. Anna looked down over the barrier to her right and slowed down a little, there was no need for speed here and although the metal barriers looked strong, there was no need to test them.

The hills sloped upwards to the other side, mostly dry, brown scrubland with the occasional large crumbling orange rock penetrating the soil.

It looked like they were just about as high as they were going to get now and the road had begun to snake and curve as it hugged the contours of the cliffs and hills.

Joe was silent at the back still. "How are you getting on back there?" Anna called. "You want to take a break?"

"No. I'm fine." Came the reply. Anna could hear the tension in his voice clearly in her head.

They rounded a sharp bend. As they did, loose stones popped and bounced out from under the tyres. One sharp, marble-sized one sailed under the barrier and out into the void.

The road was dropping away quite steeply now and Anna had to keep squeezing the brakes to keep their speed under control. To the left, the banks and hills gave way to a sheer cliff above them.

They passed a sign warning of falling rocks. Joe glanced up nervously and hung on tighter as they descended the road which had been cut out of the hillside.

Suddenly, like a camera-flash in reverse an instant of darkness burst in front of Joe's vision. He flinched.

"What is it?" Anna yelled, bringing the moped to a gentle stop. They got off, she was keen to stop anyhow; this road was making her very nervous.

"I think I had a flashback or something. It was just an instant." He put his palms to the sides of his head. He hadn't spontaneously *felt* anything since he had appeared, but now his head was beginning to pound. "I think I saw this exact road, but at night. It was hard to tell."

"So you *did* come this way then." She took her bag from her shoulder, pulled out a bottle and took a long drink. The sun was starting to get hot, even though it was only a little after ten. "Are you okay to go on? I'll go slowly in case it happens again."

"I think it will." He climbed on behind Anna and they moved on at a much slower pace. Looking down, they saw the road bend sharp right at the bottom then disappear again around an outcrop of cliff. Joe had an uneasy feeling about that place, but given the state of the road that wasn't entirely unreasonable.

The brakes squealed as they reached the bottom of the hill. The cliffs towered up to the left and evidence of rockfalls could be seen along the wide margin beside the road itself. Anna gasped as they turned the hairpin. The edge to the right fell away to ragged rocks jutting from the sea below.

Joe's sense of unease ramped up, then the dark flash happened again, this time randomly flickering such that he was sure now that he was seeing the same road at night. He was rounding this bend, tearing down the hill and breaking hard. The rear of motorcycle fishtailed as he gunned the engine again and sped upwards toward the left turn– it stopped.

"Stop!" he yelled. Anna pulled the bike to a stop again halfway up the incline to the blind bend ahead of them. "It's somewhere near here. The flashbacks are coming fast now."

"We should walk." she suggested. The bend was about 50 or 60 metres ahead. Anna got off and started pushing the moped up the hill. Joe walked on ahead with his palm to his forehead. The throbbing was getting stronger.

"It's that bend isn't it?" Anna said, voice shaking. "You went right over the edge didn't you? Oh God, this is awful."

They walked on for a couple of minutes, Anna was close to tears with the thought of Joe and Charlie's accidents.

"No, no. Stop. We need to go back a little." Joe suddenly cried. "It's not the bend. It's a little way before."

They backtracked, then Joe stood stock-still by the road. Frozen in place, staring over the edge. There was a small gap in the barrier, not recently damaged judging by the way that grass and a small bush had grown up against the twisted metal.

"This is it." Joe said with certainty. "I just saw it. I

saw my bike go over the edge here."

"That's why they never found you." Anna whispered. She found her voice again slowly, "They would have been looking for a fresh accident spot. This looks like it happened years ago. Why didn't they fix it?"

"Rabbit." Joe said. "I swerved to avoid a rabbit." He was standing close to the edge now, peering down. At this point, the drop wasn't sheer, it was a series of broken rocks and fissures with trees and bushes grimly clinging on.

"We should call the police." Anna said. "Tell them this is where the accident was."

"They'd never believe you. You have no proof." He turned to her, a look of determination on his face now. "They would have checked along this road if they knew I'd come this way. They won't look again without a good reason."

"So, what do we do. I was hoping all you needed to do was find your death-place."

"I think I need to be buried. Properly." He reached out and touched her hand. "We need to know for sure that I'm down there."

"But that's certain death, I can't climb down there. Look how unstable those rocks are. There's no way."

"I'll go." said Joe flatly. "I'm already dead."

"But how–"

"I don't have any weight. I can climb down easily, those loose rocks won't budge." He turned and eyed up the steep slope upwards on the other side. "Let's see."

He walked over and deftly climbed up the broken boulders at the foot of the slope, then pulled himself up higher without any trouble at all. He was about two stories up when he called down.

"Watch." He let go of the branch of the bush he was holding onto and fell. Anna screamed, but he dropped slowly, bumping gently against the side of the hill and the rocks as if he were a balloon.

He landed next to Anna light as a feather, "See, I'll be fine."

"You complete git!" she yelled at him. "Why didn't you tell me you were going to do that."

"Sorry, you're right. Come on, let's get this done while I'm still feeling brave."

Joe pushed through the broken barrier, past the branches of the bush growing around it. They moved slightly as he passed through and Anna could see that some of the branches had indeed been freshly broken. But on the miles of road here, it would have been very easy to overlook.

Joe had moved down a fair way now and was approaching a collection of huge boulders that must have fallen years ago, or been pushed aside as the road was built.

"I think it's just a little further down." he called back. I'm going to climb over these big rocks.

Anna pushed the bush aside a little to get a better view, but wished she hadn't and stepped back behind the intact part of the barrier. Joe was hanging onto the branch of a sickly looking tree as he climbed over the rock. His hand seemed to slip and he vanished over the edge.

"Joe!" she called. "What happened?"

His voice came back, faint, fearful, "Anna, help! I

slipped, my hand... it went through the branch, I'm starting to fade again."

"You're too far away from me!" she called over the edge, "You shouldn't have let the rocks get between us." There was silence. "Joe?"

He had managed to grab hold of a root and was dangling over the side of the large rock. Below, a fall of about fifteen feet to a jumble of smaller, broken rocks. He knew that the fall wouldn't hurt him but, "Help, I'm slipping. If I fall any further I'm going to fade even more! I might not even be able to get back." As he spoke, his hand started to slide into and through the thick root. He scrabbled with his feet but they felt slippery and he couldn't get a purchase.

"I don't know what to do." she yelled, fingering her hair nervously. "I can't see you."

Joe shifted his position to try to grab the root with his other hand but it slid right through and he fell.

He landed on the rocks below, unhurt of course, but he could feel himself slipping from the world itself. He tried to stand, but it was like trying to stand in mud. His hands and feet were slipping into the pile of freshly fallen rocks and stones.

As he scrabbled to right himself his hand touched something just below the mush of stones and gravel. It hit him like a bolt of lightning and he was suddenly in the dark speeding along the road. An animal, a rabbit maybe darted into the road, eyes flaring in the beam of his headlight. He swerved, crashed against the barrier and slid along until he reached a gap and fell through, tumbling down with his bike onto a boulder. It tipped and fell taking Joe and his bike down the side of the slope onto a ledge. The rock shattered and a cascade of smaller rocks, soil and stones rained down on him burying him. All was silent and dark. He knew he had died.

Gradually, as if waking from a dream, light seeped back into Joe's vision, a sound, echoing in his head. His name being called. It was Anna.

"I'm okay. I found it – me, I found my body. It's down here, buried in the rocks."

"I can see you." Anna called. He looked up and saw her hanging over the side a little further down where the rock was undisturbed. But how had she gotten down?

Joe's hand fell back down to his side where he lay, it touched the thing that he had felt earlier. He had a little substance now that he was in sight of Anna and reached into the gravel to grasp it. With all his willpower, he pulled the object free from the soil and stones. It was a cap, battered and dirty, but it was *his* cap, he knew it.

"Joe, quickly! Climb back up, I can't hold on much longer." Anna shouted from above. Joe pulled his wits together. Clutching the cap, he hefted himself back up the slope, taking a different route up to try to keep Anna in sight, to keep the connection to her that gave him a presence here on Earth.

As he neared the top, he felt himself lighter, more connected with the rocks and roots that he grabbed and pulled at. Anna heaved herself back up and over the side of the barrier weeping, dirt streaked down her face with tears.

They collapsed together, exhausted, they kissed long

and hungrily holding each other tighter than ever until the tears subsided into a numb sort of shock.

"We did it." Joe breathed eventually, "We found where I died, we can prove it." The cap had dropped through his fingers to the ground. Anna picked it up and turned it about in her hands. It was the same design as the one in the photograph in the paper, though she would never have known that it was red.

She looked inside to see if maybe he had written his name; her whole frame sagged with sadness. The white band inside was stained with dried blood. No name, but the DNA would be all the proof they needed that this was where the mortal remains of Joe Brooks lay.

"The cliff collapsed after I skidded over." Joe said quietly; he'd seen Anna looking at the stain. "The rubble buried me and my bike. There's no way they would have found me."

The coffee at the police station was surprisingly good, though Anna wasn't quite the authority on police station coffee. They'd tried to do all they could to make her comfortable while they made arrangements to notify Joe's parents and recover the body. The little interview room was pretty much what she'd expected it to be, plain white walls, table with metal chairs either side, interview recording machine. She smiled sheepishly at the camera in the corner of the room by the ceiling.

A pair of officers had already set off to Joe's parents to identify the cap. The line that she was a pen friend trying to track down his last movements had been taken in, so she was officially on board for the whole ride.

In lieu of lunch, Anna had happily accepted a plate of pastries scrounged from the canteen and was brushing the last of the crumbs from her front when there was a sharp knock on the door.

Lieutenant Babin's head appeared around the door. "Miss Wilder. Hope you're comfortable," he began in excellent English, "My apologies again, but we're only the *Police Municipale*, we only handle small affairs locally. Someone from the *Police Nationale* will be here in a few minutes to oversee. They will be bringing the equipment needed to recover the young gentleman."

Joe was sitting opposite Anna, nervously tapping the table, though of course it only served to distract her.

He cleared his throat politely, "I know that you have already agreed to come along to assist in pinpointing the location, but are you *absolutely* sure that is your wish?"

She nodded resolutely. "Yes, please. It would mean a lot to me."

"Okay, then. Thank you. I will arrange for a car and we can set off in just a few minutes. Please. Just wait here." He nodded politely and left.

Anna had avoided talking with Joe in the interview room. She'd always seen these places in movies and on TV where the room was monored and recorded. It would look a little odd. Joe shrugged back at her and resumed his nervous tapping.

"Yes, just here." Anna leaned forward and pointed to the spot where the concealed break in the barrier was.

"*Oh la vache!* How have you found this?" Babin

exclaimed, stopping the car and switching on the flashing warning lights. "I travel this road, maybe once every week."

The *gardien* at the back jumped out and began setting out cones and tape to warn oncoming traffic of the impending operation. Joe quickly slipped out before the door closed.

"I think I was just lucky?" Anna ventured. But Babin was impressed, not suspicious.

"Indeed, very lucky. But for us all, I think. Please, remain inside the car until we have completed making the road safe."

A couple of minutes later, a recovery truck arrived and positioned itself with the help of the *gardien* from her car. Two men and a woman emerged and began busying themselves with the winch equipment.

Anna turned around to see what else was happening; it had quickly become very busy, with a full road block now in place. An unmarked car arrived and was waved into the area by a police officer with a radio. It stopped behind her car and two police, clearly of high rank got out and began talking with Babin.

While they were talking, he looked over at Anna – they were talking about her. She jumped when she turned back to see Joe's face pressed against the window. He had a serious expression.

It seemed more or less safe to get out now; there didn't appear to be any more vehicles arriving.

"It's all happening now isn't it?" she said to Joe.

"There's two people in the back of that car." he said quietly, eyeing the vehicle.

Discretely, she turned to face the car and, to the side,

the police bigwigs. They now seemed to be discussing the removal of the body with a significant amount of Gallic arm-waving. The windows were quite dark, but Anna could make out two people in the back seat.

"Ah. Yes, of course." she said awkwardly. "Your parents, I presume."

"Must be," he said moving a little closer.

"Do you recognise them?" she said behind her hand.

"No, I'm not getting anything yet."

One of the men from the recovery vehicles shouted. He was dressed in forensic overalls with a climbing helmet and harness. Babin called over to Anna, "Can you please move over here now. They are ready to attempt the recovery."

Anna and Joe complied. She smiled at the senior officers, but they just returned stony expressions and grunted acknowledgement.

More shouts from the recovery team and the man in the harness slowly stepped over the edge and lowered himself down. Everything was silent for several minutes. It seemed as if everyone was holding their breath. Then came a series of indistinct calls, echoed on the radio of the woman at the top. She picked up a control pad from the truck and watched as a cable and hook slowly lowered itself from an a-frame they had erected over the cliff edge.

Anna looked at Joe to see him transfixed by the scene, grim-faced.

The radio squawked again – unintelligible at this distance – and the winch motor restarted. The engine of the truck revved a little, providing additional power to the motor. As the cable took up slack, the frame creaked under the weight of the load being lifted.

The winch motor whined on and in time, an object could be seen cresting the edge of the cliff, rising up into the air.

The car doors behind them flew open "Joe, oh God no." his mother cried as she ran towards the recovery scene. Babin and another officer held her back, while her husband tried his best to soothe her.

Anna turned back to the winch and gasped at the sight of Joe's mangled motorcycle turning gently in the breeze. It was crushed and broken, parts of the faring were hanging off and the front wheel buckled nearly in two. She put her hands to her mouth. Joe still remained resolutely silent, eyes locked on the wreckage.

With a degree of manipulation, the ruined motorbike was dragged back to the road and laid to one side for later removal, possibly examination. The garbled voice that sounded on the radio could mean only one thing – they were ready to lift the body.

"You don't need to watch this." Joe said quietly, the sudden voice made her shiver. The voice of the poor boy that lay broken and dead on the ledge below – the voice of her love.

She kept her gaze forward, hands still clapped to her mouth, "I'm okay." she managed, then lowered her hands, readying herself for what was surely to come.

They had attached a basket-like stretcher similar the ones Anna had seen on TV dangling under helicopters. Down it went over the side, out of view until the motor stopped again.

Joe's mother began to sob quietly. Anna wanted to

say something, but they hadn't been introduced, she didn't even know if the police had told them who she was or what her part in all this was.

Joe put his hand in hers and she grabbed it, squeezing it hard. They both stood there in silence. The cable wobbled and swayed from time to time as the man at the bottom worked.

Finally, the movement stopped and that voice again over the radio. It was curt, clipped this time.

The winch started up again for the last time with its grizzly cargo.

Behind him, Joe could hear his mother sobbing again as the cable wound up and up. He glanced backwards to the grief-stricken couple that he knew were his parents but now were just strangers standing in the road. A bumping sound made him look back to the operation at the cliff edge.

Suddenly, like a dazzling sun bursting over the edge of the cliff, the stretcher appeared. Silvery light flowed out from it in waves, so incredibly bright but it didn't hurt his eyes.

"Anna, do you see the light?" he gasped.

"What light?" she shuddered, she was staring at the stretcher swinging gently at the apex of the frame. This was Joe. They'd found him at last. A gurney was wheeled up to the side of the road and the stretcher containing a crumpled black body bag was hefted atop.

This was too much for Joe's mother. She broke away and ran wailing towards the body of her son.

The police felt that it was best not to interfere for a moment and allowed her to pass through where she threw herself on the body, head on the chest area weeping.

Joe too felt drawn to the body, the light had warmth, he hadn't felt warmth for so long and he craved it with all his being. Breaking hand contact, he started walking slowly towards the light and his body.

"Joe?" Anna whispered. But he didn't hear her.

"Yes, it's Joe." A deep, kindly voice by her side. She looked up and saw Joe's father standing by her. "I can't find words to say how grateful we are that you found him." He put a hand on her upper arm, "Come, if you need to take a moment with him before they take him away." He waked slowly to be with his wife to join her in her desperate grief.

Anna followed and stood next to where Joe had stopped.

"The light, Anna. It's here for me at last." he whispered, serenely.

"Joe–" she choked.

"I remember now." he said simply. "My life, all of it. I was so lucky. But Anna, there's more, *afterwards*. I know why I was sent to you. I was with Charlie, I spoke with him and he has a message for you."

Anna dissolved into tears, "You were *there?*" she managed.

"Yes. His spirit was in the hospital, I joined him and he wanted to speak to you but he couldn't find a way. You were there in the room with him and he couldn't make you hear him."

From Joe's perspective, the light pouring from the body started to waver, the overpowering brightness was fading; now filaments of light could be seen twisting and warping from the source. They were starting to bend and writhe, like vines almost, searching for something.

"What did he say?" she whispered, trembling, tears rolling down her face. There was a moment's pause. She turned her head to look towards him and her heart froze. He was standing, motionless, arms starting to rise up slightly. Now she could just about detect a faint light from the body. Joe's parents were standing now, hugging as the coroners were lifting the stretcher away.

The glow became a little more distinct and Anna thought she could see threads of light waving in the air, stretching towards Joe. As she watched, they gently wrapped themselves about him, almost lovingly, caressing his body before folding more tightly. He lifted up off his feet a few inches.

Anna took a step back staring at Joe, now engulfed in the ethereal tendrils.

Joe's parents had turned to see what Anna was looking at. They saw nothing of course. His mother started to speak but Babin, who had joined them stopped her.

"No." He said quietly, "Leave her for a moment."

"What's happening?" Joe's Father asked, watching Anna standing, staring into space.

"*Quelque chose d'incroyable...*" Babin whispered in awe. He waved to the others to keep their distance and the coroners to step back from the gurney.

"What did he say?" Anna repeated. But Joe had lifted up a little further and was starting to tip back slightly. "Joe!" she cried, oblivious to everyone else nearby,

"You can't leave now, you can't!" But he began to drift slowly towards the body, the light emanating from it had begun to strengthen, growing brighter as he drew closer, more ivory white tendrils reached out to wrap around him until he had become a blurred shape of light, losing his distinctiveness until eventually Anna couldn't tell him from the light at all.

Then gently, and softly the light ceased.

Anna slumped to her knees. One of the coroners made to help her but Babin held a hand up to halt her. He walked slowly to her and crouched, gently placing a hand on her back between her shoulders. Her body heaved with heavy sobs and it was some time before she was able to form words.

"He's gone." She rasped and raised her head to look at Babin.

"Yes." he said kindly. "He's at peace now. You have played your part in this admirably."

She looked up at him quizzically, "You knew?"

She saw the police officer now in a very different light, as if he were someone completely different now, gone was the stern, official look of the regional lieutenant of police; his face was full of sadness, the kind that is ingrained over decades, worn into the skin by experience like weathered sandstone.

"I did. I could see him when you arrived at the police station." His voice was low; this was a conversation only for the two of them.

Her face relaxed, there was relief there, "You saw him all this time?"

"Right up to the end, *oui*." He looked over to where the coroners were now preparing to load the gurney into the van. Joe's parents were talking with the two police officials and sounds of disassembly had begun at the cliff face. "It was beautiful." A silvery line of moisture had formed at the lower lids of his eyes.

"Why didn't you tell me?" She was curious, not angry.

"This was for you and you alone. I cannot interfere." He offered his hand, "Here, let me help you."

She took his hand and got unsteadily to her feet.

"I'm sorry that you didn't get your message." he said, "This must be like losing someone twice."

She pulled a wad of napkins from her bag, wiped her eyes and blew her nose. "Three times." She looked over to see the coroner's van door close. "Twice for Charlie and again for Joe."

Joe's parents appeared to be finishing their conversation. "Do you mind if I speak with them?"

"No. Please. Go ahead. Though..." He paused, "They might not understand what has just happened. It might be easier if you, um–"

"It's okay," she said, "I'm kind of used to this now. I can put a spin on it."

Babin nodded, "Thank you. It would be easier for everyone. And again, my most profound sympathies."

She made her way over to Joe's parents, who smiled tearfully at her.

"I understand that we owe you a debt of gratitude." Her Father said. He held out his hand to shake, "Harvey."

She took his hand, "Anna." she said, a little nervously.

"And my wife Pamala."

"Call me Pam." They exchanged polite handshakes,

"I can't imagine how you managed to find him. You must have known him so well." A look of sadness swept across her face, "We hardly knew him this past year. When he went missing…" She trailed off into her thoughts.

Harvey picked it up, "Yes, we had no idea where he went. These last months have been torture. The police did their best, but they just ran out of ideas." He took a breath to collect himself, "But now it's all settled, the uncertainty is over."

They talked for some time about Joe. Anna learned a little about his former life and they about hers.

Around them the road was returned to normal, as if all this had never happened. Another truck appeared to replace the winch truck and workers began repairing the barrier.

Babin quietly slipped away to his car and dialled an international number on his mobile. He waited for the call to connect, looking out of the windscreen at Anna talking with Mr and Mrs Brooks. "Ah. Monsieur Felton? Lieutenant Babin here. Montpellier Police. We need to talk."

CHAPTER 13

ANNA

HER ROOM WAS cold. A sickly December afternoon light struggled through the window and cast more of a gloom than illumination.

She didn't bother to turn the light on. Her luggage obstinately tipped over and fell as she let go of the handle. She looked at it with dead eyes, shucked off her trainers and fell backwards onto her bed.

The flight back had been the loneliest time she could ever remember. Crammed into the middle seat with strangers all around. She had pretended to sleep until the drinks came around. Two cans of G&T. The flight attendant saw her red eyes and served her without question. Booze wasn't going to be the answer, but for now it muted some of the questions circling around in her head.

The house was quiet as always. Sam was probably out at work, or at the Gym or having a life somewhere. She stared at a twist of dusty cobweb hanging from the ceiling above her. She had nothing now, nobody. No job and most likely thrown off her university course by now. Her life was utterly derailed.

Joe had come and gone. Life was exciting for a while. She managed a grim smile at some of the good moments. Even the arguments were better than the void that faced her right now; there was life and connection to another living– no, Joe was dead. He'd always been dead. So was Charlie – the only other person in this world that she had been able to really talk with.

The sound of a car pulling up in front of the house made her stir from the bed. She drifted to the window and looked out. It was Sam, or at least her bum, sticking out from the car as she collected some bags from the back seat. She glanced up at Anna at the window and jumped, dropping one of her bags.

The front door opened as Anna got to the bottom of the stairs.

"Shit, girl!" she squealed "I thought you were a ghost! Nearly had a stroke." She dropped her bags to the floor and launched herself into one of her trademark hugs."

Anna went with the hug, but she was still dead inside.

"You look like crap. Are you okay, where did you go? I haven't seen you for... what, a week?"

"I..." she didn't know what to say, "I went on a little holiday." But there was no joy in her voice.

"Holiday? Ohhh... With this Joe Guy?" She scanned Anna's face. This wasn't the face of someone who'd just had a banger of a holiday with their fit new boyfriend. "Oh. Shit. You broke up?" she guessed.

"He's dead."

It seemed like time had stopped. There was no other way to put it. Sam was utterly thrown and just stood, mouth slightly parted trembling imperceptibly.

"De– No. How? What happ–"

"Motorbike accident." Anna continued, almost matter of factly, "Went over a cliff." She mimed a drop and explosion with her hand. It was shaking.

"No no no, that's impossible. That's how–"

"Charlie died. Yep. Same thing."

Sam's eyes were brimming with tears but right now, Anna was beyond tears. She just felt utterly empty.

Sam broke the silence again, "Look, babe. I know that there's nothing that I can do to fix this. But there's one thing I can do that might just take the edge off."

"Your chilli?" Anna said.

"My Chilli. You look like you've not eaten for days."

"I don't think I ate since breakfast yesterday."

"Right. Let's get you fed." Sam picked up the bags of shopping and headed to the kitchen. "Grab that last one will you?"

Anna stooped to get the last bag, it clinked invitingly.

Sam turned back and smiled, "...and wine. Then chocolate!"

This was the Sam she remembered from before the world ended, "Sam, I think you just saved my life." *I think she really did*, she thought to herself.

Sam had insisted that they didn't talk about the 'serious issues' until they had eaten and at least one of those bottles was empty. So, they had spent a happy time cooking together, complaining about the weather, the rent increase and a dozen other mind-fillers until they were properly fed and wondering where they had put the bottle opener.

"So," Sam snapped off two rows of Cadbury's Dark Milk and handed it over to Anna, "You ready?"

Sam was clever. So very very clever. The heating was on, the brain chemicals from the capsaicin in the food, the chocolate and half a bottle of supermarket

Merlot had developed the most wonderful sense of wellbeing.

"Okay." she said, nodding slowly. "But let me finish completely before you say anything."

She told her *everything*. How he appeared to her, the initial conflict, falling in love. Sam's eyes widened when she heard about the sex and nearly choked over the encounter in the airplane bathroom.

By the time she had described how Joe had passed on, they both were reaching for the strategically placed box of tissues.

It was an incredible story. But a large part of Sam's mind couldn't quite get over the literal incredulity of the whole tale. 'Depressed room mate vanishes for days, comes back saying boyfriend that nobody had seen was a ghost and now he's dead' – or whatever that means.

Sam had known Anna for years and she had a good sense for when something wasn't right with her. She decided to go along with it for now. Anna had clearly brightened her mood, getting this story off her chest looked like a great unburdening. Let her enjoy that while she could.

But truthfully, Sam thought, her best friend needed help.

Anna drained her glass. "I need to pee!" She announced triumphantly, and marched out.

I'll speak with someone in the morning. Sam said to herself.

There was a buzzing sound and Anna's phone started ringing. No sign of her yet. She answered it.

"Hello, is that Anna?" A man's voice.

"Um, no she's out of the room at the moment, can I take a message?"

"Oh, yes, thanks. It's Harvey Brooks, Joe's father. Sorry, who is this?"

"It's Samantha, I'm Anna's housemate." *Joe's Father!*

"Ah, good. Yes, I just wanted to say that Joe's funeral has been set for next Tuesday. We're going to be flying back to the UK tomorrow with the body. We'd love it if Anna could be there seeing as she was so close to him."

Sam's mouth was agape, "Er, yes. Thank you, I'll let her know."

"Wonderful, thanks Samantha. I'll text the details over when we're back in the UK."

He hung up.

Well. That changed things. The whole story wasn't made up. But shit, the wine was getting to her, that really meant... Anna walked back into the room, grinning and carrying a bottle.

Sam stared at her like a returning hero, "You *really* had sex with a ghost? How does *THAT* work?"

The trees lining the path to the entrance of the church had already dropped most of their leaves, but those that remained burst with golden colour through the bright morning sunlight. The cloudless sky threw a brilliant crisp backdrop to the scene.

Joe's coffin progressed slowly up the path, the pall-bearers grim-faced, top-hatted and dignified. A gentle gust of wind sent a brilliantly coloured confetti of leaves spiralling down to the path – some lingered on the smooth wood then slid to the ground.

The mourners inside stood as the coffin was brought inside and set in place.

Anna wasn't the religious type, but she found the service immensely moving. The hymns were mostly unfamiliar to her, but joe's parents had brought in a small choir to bolster the uncertain cantillations of the assembled family and friends. It was beautiful.

The family had a plot at the church. At the end, the coffin was carried outside where the grave has been prepared. Anna hung back from the group gathered around the grave itself and watched as the final words were said.

"Nice day for it, huh?" said a voice to her side; low and respectful. Anna hadn't noticed anyone standing next to her. She glanced over and barely caught herself from shouting.

"Fu– *Joe*, what are you doing here?" she breathed.

"Oh, I wouldn't miss this for the world." he said with a cheeky grin. "Look, we'd better go over there in the trees behind that big mausoleum thing. Bad form to be seen chatting with the stiff at a funeral."

She glanced back at the group to make sure nobody was watching and slipped quietly away out of sight and earshot.

Anna threw her arms around Joe and pulled him tightly to her, she kissed him, feeling his silky skin against her mouth. But something had changed subtly, the feeling was just as intense, but the kiss, the embrace had the feeling of deep and profound friendship, it had a mellowness that she'd not felt before. Like a fine wine, perhaps? The lustiness of weeks past had matured in the days they had been apart, leaving her feeling truly satisfied and happy when they pulled apart and looked at each other.

"How have you been managing since – you know?" he asked.

"I thought I was going to die at first. Sam came back – thought I was a ghost!" They laughed at the irony. "We've connected again really well. I,... I think I'm feeling okay now. But God I missed you." She pulled him close again, just to feel connected to him. She felt something rustle in her pocket and pulled it out. "Your dad gave me this. Said to open it when I got home."

Joe rolled his eyes, "I think you'd better open it now." he said.

She ripped the envelope open. There was a beautifully hand-written letter and, "A cheque. For– HOW MUCH? What? No, they can't."

"That's just like them. Splashing the cash. You know, they're really grateful that you helped find me. It's just their only way to express themselves. Honestly, take the money, they can afford it. Hopefully it'll help get you through Uni."

"Um, and a new car and a deposit for a place of my own... this is silly money."

"Not to them." He kissed her on the forehead. "You have to realise that I'm not here to stay, you know I can't, right."

"Yeah." She looked down at his chest then back into his silvery eyes, "I guess so."

"I figured something out too." Joe said. Anna looked up into his eyes, "Since the library, I wondered why

I didn't appear to you until months after. Then it dawned on me. You weren't saving *me*. It was *me* that saved *you* in the end."

Anna knew right away what he meant. The weeks and months after Charlie had died, she had been slowly descending into depression, losing herself. "You're right." she admitted, "I don't know how much longer I'd have been able to go on like that. You pulled me back from my own cliff edge." She laid her head on his chest, "Thank you Joe."

"I didn't quite finish everything I'd been sent here for though. Kind of got dragged away, didn't I?"

"Oh–" She remembered Babin, "Did you know that French policeman, Babin, he could *see* you?"

"No, but I did afterwards. He's not alone, there are others. I don't think I'm supposed to let on though, but they're okay. If they do get in touch with you *trust* them."

"I don't understand?"

"Don't worry, I think they'll let you get on with things now that I've crossed over. But hey, back to business – that message."

"From Charlie? Oh, God. What did he say?"

"Really, it was just very simple, but he needed you to... well, maybe it's best he tells you himself." He gestured over her shoulder, "I brought a guest." She turned around, and there – right there was Charlie.

He was all silvery glass like Joe, but it was Charlie.

"Hey Sis." he said, beaming.

She looked back to Joe and mouthed "Thank you" before running at her dear brother and hugging him as if her life depended on it.

"Oh, Charlie. I've been in bits since you died."

"I'm sorry, I really am. I wanted to tell you how much I loved you at the hospital, but I just couldn't make myself heard. It almost drove me crazy watching you sitting there day and night in that chair. I just wanted to tell you not to worry, that I loved you."

Tears of joy and sadness and relief streamed down Anna's face.

"Forgive me for being so bloody stupid that night. I know I shouldn't have gone out on that bike. I know I tore you and mum and dad apart that night."

"Oh, Charlie, of course I forgive you, you pillock!" she laughed.

He smiled at her, his face calm now "Thanks, sis." he said peacefully.

"Okay chappie," Joe said joining him, "It's time – we've done our finale."

A beautiful light began to shine from nowhere in particular, as if the trees, the grass, even the air had begun to glow with a soft warm light.

"Thanks for finding me," Joe said, his voice becoming distant as the light slowly engulfed the two visitors. "I love you."

Then, as if it had never happened at all, the light was gone.

THE END

Thanks for reading!
We hope you enjoyed this book. If you did then please consider leaving a review at Amazon – it would mean a lot to us all.

OTHER TITLES FROM

SCI-FI-CAFE

Available to buy in paperback and eBook from
Amazon and other good online stores.
Scan the affiliate links in the QR codes to find out
more about each book.

The Girl from the Temple Ruins

A temple to the goddess Amalishah lies in the remotest wastelands of Assyria. She is their protector but to others she is known as The Monster.

The Hittite prince Artaxias visits the Palace of the Goddess to implore the temple priests to free prisoners captured from the border. He knows their fate, the appalling human sacrifice that will be made to the goddess who must feed on human blood.

Four thousand years have eroded the memory and the evidence of these events until British archaeologist Michael Townsend discovers the subterranean lair of the goddess. Michael is visited and instantly captivated by a mysterious and beautiful woman. The Hittites called her monster, a creature now called vampire.

ISBN: 978-1-910779-41-5

City of Storms

When top foreign correspondent Sean Brian flies into Manila in the Philippines, a typhoon and a political revolution are uppermost in his thoughts.

But what also awaits will turn his already busy life into a roller coaster of romance, adventure, elation and despair.

At the centre of this transformation is an infant boy child, born, abandoned and plunged into street poverty in the grim underbelly of an Asian metropolis.

This is the catalyst for a story ranging from the corrupt, violent world of back street city sex clubs and drug addiction, to the clean air of the Sulu Sea and the South Pacific; from the calm safety of an island paradise to the violent guerilla world of the notorious Golden Triangle and the southern Philippines archipelago.

As we follow the child, Bagyo, into fledgling manhood, we can only wonder at the ripples that spread from one individual to engulf so many others – and at the injustice that still corrodes life on the mean streets of the world.

ISBN: 978-1-908387-99-8